CLEMENTINE LOVES RED

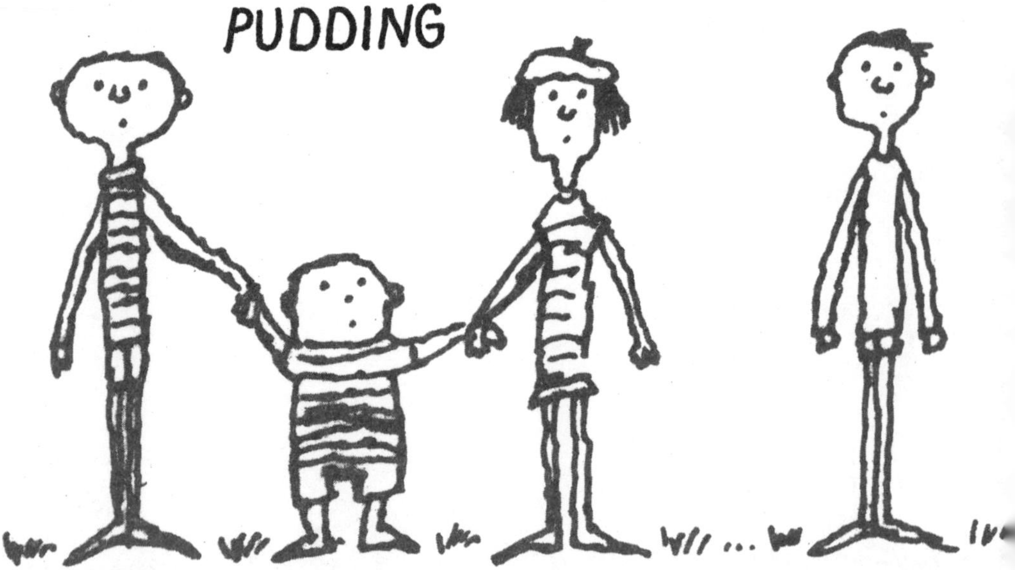
MARK
PUDDING
ANNIE
TEDDY

CLEMENTINE LOVES RED

Krystyna Boglar

ILLUSTRATED BY

Bohdan Butenko

TRANSLATED BY

Zosia Krasodomska-Jones

& Antonia Lloyd-Jones

PUSHKIN CHILDREN'S BOOKS

EDDIE

FREDDIE

MACADAMIA

Pushkin Press
71–75 Shelton Street
London, WC2H 9JQ

Original text © Krystyna Boglar, 1970
Illustrations © Bohdan Butenko, 1970
English translation © Antonia Lloyd-Jones and Zosia Krasodomska-Jones

Published by arrangement with Wydawnictwo Dwie Siostry, Warsaw (Poland).

Clementine Loves Red was first published as *Klementyna lubi kolor czerwony*
in Warsaw, 1970

First published by Pushkin Children's Books in 2017

9 8 7 6 5 4 3 2 1

ISBN 9781782691181

Text designed and typeset by Tetragon, London

Printed in Poland by W. L. Anczyca S.A., Krakow

www.pushkinpress.com

In which we find Macadamia and
lose our peace of mind

===

IT WAS SATURDAY, THE 26TH OF AUGUST. WHY THIS date is so important will become clear later on, but let's just say for now that this particular Saturday was extremely long and boring. And yet nobody found the prospect of an early night at all amusing. But what else is there to do in a small cottage at the edge of the forest after dark? Of course, grown-ups always find a solution to the problem, but what about children? And what about hens, for instance? Hens are a good example here, because, as everyone knows, in the countryside you "go to bed with the hens". And this was a village in the countryside, with the very ordinary name of St Jude's, but everyone called it the Holiday Hamlet:

IN THE COUNTRYSIDE YOU

Mum, Dad and even chubby Mrs Clotted Cream, with whom they were staying. Of course, she had a proper name too, but "Mrs Clotted Cream" was one of Annie's brilliant ideas, because Mrs Clotted Cream provided all the holidaymakers in the area with delicious, thick cream—a mightily important addition to wild strawberries and cheesecake.

And even though it wasn't a "cheesecake day", this particular Saturday was to be a very important day in the lives of Mark, Annie and Pudding. Pudding (though with some difficulty) was sitting on top of the fence

8

"GO TO BED WITH THE HENS"

that separated the chicken coop from the sunflower patch, lazily swinging his legs as he shelled tiny seeds picked straight off the head of a sunflower standing stiffly beside him. Mrs Clotted Cream was very annoyed about it, because almost all the sunflowers had had their best bits nibbled away and the bald patches were conspicuously ugly, but Pudding was so greedy that not even his dad's scolding could stop him.

So there he was, sitting on the fence, which was creaking ominously, and he was wondering what he would do tomorrow. After all, when you're on holiday

9

Sundays are really no different from any other day of the week.

"What do you think?" he asked, spitting out a seed shell. "Will it be boiled chicken for dinner again tomorrow?"

"You can bet it will," replied Mark, furiously scratching his mosquito-savaged calves.

Mark hated boiled chicken, but in this small village surrounded by woods, thirty kilometres from the nearest town, there was nothing else to be had. With a big yawn he glanced up above the tall pine trees, tinged red by the setting sun.

"Shall we run over to the Frog King?"

"We can walk there," said Pudding, scrambling off the fence. "I don't really feel like running!"

Perhaps we should explain that Pudding was really called Derek, but no one ever used that name any more, not even Mum, who used to be mad about it. Nor was there anything odd about the fact that the nickname "Pudding" had stuck to him so easily. For as long as anyone could remember, Pudding had always been plump and wasn't fond of moving. So Mark just sighed and nodded.

"Shall we fetch Annie?" he asked, just to be polite,

because they both knew they always went to see the Frog King in a threesome.

Annie had just finished her evening ritual of watering the flower beds and was putting the empty watering can away beside the water butt.

"Let's go!" said Mark, sniffing the air.

For wafting through the open kitchen window came the aroma of plum tart.

"Don't even think about it," said Annie, shaking her hands dry. "We've no chance of a single crumb of it today!"

"Why exactly is it that you can only have cakes on Sundays?" complained Pudding. "It's so unfair!"

All three of them agreed wholeheartedly. Because really, why are such delicious treats as plum tart or walnut cake always baked on a Saturday? And why can they only be eaten on a Sunday?

The children breathed in the smell of the tart once more, and then slowly toddled off in single file towards the small pond, which was surrounded by a dark-green wall of forest.

They had discovered the pond—or the Frog King's empire—by accident, early on in their stay at the Holiday

Hamlet. While playing Red Indians, with the requisite feathers stuck in their messy hair, they had scattered about the forest in search of Eddie—or Green Arrow—who was hiding somewhere in the undergrowth. Suddenly, a loud scream and a splash had rung out from the left of a huge oak tree, enough to lure Pudding, who that day was acting as camp sentry, out of the wigwam. It had turned out to be Freddie, the Great Cockroach in person, Indian chief and warrior supreme, who had just sunk up to his neck in the duckweed-coated pond. They had combined forces to fish him out, and as he was casting off his drenched clothes, a huge, green frog had leapt out of his shirt pocket.

Naturally, that was the Frog King—the ruler of the bottomless pond, the king whose realm, though not large, was extremely rich in froggy citizens. He even had his own frog choir, which gave splendid evening concerts.

And so they were marching along in single file, with Mark leading the way, until suddenly he stopped in his tracks. Of course, Pudding went crashing into him and only narrowly avoided knocking him over.

"What's up?" asked Annie, bringing up the rear.

"Shhh..." whispered Mark, clearly listening to something.

"I'm sssscared," stammered Pudding, just in case. Pudding always thought that if he was already frightened, then the whole problem was off his plate, because nothing scarier could possibly happen.

"Do you hear that? Someone's crying," said Mark, pointing at a clump of bushes with purple flowers. "Over there!"

Now all three of them could hear a soft sobbing noise.

"Maybe it's a ghost," said Pudding, taking a step backwards.

"Ghosts don't sob, they rattle their chains," replied Annie confidently.

"But what if it hasn't got its chains with it?" stammered Pudding, his voice trembling.

"Let's go!" commanded Mark, and began forging ahead towards the bushes.

"Mmmaybe I'll keep ggguard," mumbled Pudding, who was aching to turn tail and head for home, but Annie was just behind him on the narrow path, blocking his way.

"Come on, you coward," she said, pushing her unwilling brother ahead of her as she began to clear a path through the thorny shrubs.

Whether he liked it or not, Pudding trailed forwards, cautiously parting the branches, while struggling to control the overwhelming terror that was making his legs go weak and forcing his lip to quiver.

"I will not scream. I'm absolutely not going to scream," he told himself over and over again, as he tripped on every protruding tree root.

Meanwhile, Mark had reached the bush with the purple flowers and gently drew aside the branches.

What he saw sent him into such a spin that he didn't even react to Annie's muffled whisper, as she tugged at his sleeve, wanting to know the source of the mysterious sobbing as soon as possible.

"Well, what is it?" she asked, impatient at her brother's silence.

"What is it?" echoed Pudding.

"It's a child," said Mark hesitantly. "It's a little girl!"

"Let me see!" demanded Annie, and pushing the branches aside, she peered over Mark's shoulder.

Under the bush, on a mound of green moss, sat a little girl in floods of tears. She was wearing a red dress made of shiny material, and a small red headscarf. She pressed a dirty little fist to her mouth, from which a loud sob erupted every now and then, as her huge round eyes gazed in terror at the three unfamiliar children.

"Poor little thing," whispered Annie. "How did she come to be all alone in the forest?"

"She must have got lost," said Mark, who was also very moved by the sight of the little stranger's tear-stained face.

The girl had taken her fist out of her mouth and was listening to their conversation.

"What's your name?" asked Mark, correctly concluding that this was the only way to find out more about the child.

"Macadamia," she said in a shrill little voice.

"Macadamia?" said Annie, surprised. "But you must have a surname too? Try to remember what you're really called!"

"Macadamia!" said the girl, sounding just as shrill as before, but insistent too.

Pudding gave her a sideways look.

"If she says she's called Macadamia, then it must be true," he said firmly. "I don't have the best name either, but no one finds it strange," he added, pushing his way to the front.

"But how did you get here?" said Mark, finally getting over his surprise and deciding to take matters into his own, to his mind more experienced hands.

"From over there," whispered Macadamia, pointing to four huge oak trees standing in a row.

"From the woods?" said Pudding incredulously,

eagerly chewing a wood-sorrel leaf. "But that's the impenetrable forest!"

"That's where Clementine went!" she replied, her face crumpling. In a flash her grey eyes were filled with tears that came rolling down her little round cheeks like peas.

"Who's Clementine?" asked Pudding.

"Is she your little sister?" said Annie, full of sympathy as she knelt down beside the child and awkwardly stroked the short curls escaping from under the red headscarf.

"She's my..." the little girl sobbed loudly.

"She must be her sister," said Mark confidently, rubbing the tip of his nose.

Mark always rubbed the tip of his nose when he was in trouble, or when the problem facing him was bigger than he could handle. Meanwhile, the problem was slowly calming down, and her soft whimpers were the only sign that for Macadamia the very mention of Clementine prompted strong emotions.

"And this sister of yours just left you here in the forest?" said Pudding in surprise. He felt very sorry for the abandoned Macadamia, because, as his mother was always saying, he was soft-hearted and got very upset about other people's misfortunes. But on the other hand, he was also quite pleased that it had never occurred to his siblings to leave him alone in the dark and, at this hour of the night, particularly intimidating forest.

"She went on ahead... on her own... and then I tried to go after her..." sobbed Macadamia.

"Maybe she wanted to pick some mushrooms or wild strawberries..." said Annie, trying to find a way to justify the rather strange behaviour of the mysterious Clementine.

"But she doesn't like mushrooms!" replied the little girl, looking up at Annie with huge, startled eyes.

"She doesn't like mushrooms?!" exclaimed Mark and Pudding in chorus.

"Nnno," stammered Macadamia.

Mark was rubbing his nose harder and harder, making it turn as red as a tomato, but no brilliant ideas had come to his mind.

To be fair, we can only say that you don't very often find a little girl in the forest under some purple flowery bushes. If only Dad were here! Mark thought grumpily that Dad was always away just when he was most badly needed. And worse yet, he'd taken Mum with him!

"What are we going to do with her?" asked Annie.

Pudding shifted from foot to foot.

"Let's take her with us!"

"Of course!" said Mark. "We can't possibly leave her here!"

It was getting dark. The red glow on the pines had long since disappeared, and a cold wind was blowing through the forest. The shadows of the oak trees were getting longer and their black tentacles were reaching for the purple bush.

"Let's go!" declared Mark. As he spoke, it crossed his mind that there was still a bit of time to consider the situation that had so suddenly and unexpectedly arisen.

"Hi ho, hi ho, and homeward we will go!" shrieked Pudding, and raced ahead down the path through the brambles, happy to be heading home.

Annie took Macadamia by the hand and patiently helped her to scramble out of the thorny branches. As she did, it occurred to her that it would be good to have another girl at home. Mark and Pudding were a very good addition to family life—you could play pirates or Red Indians with them, but if you felt like doing something serious, you definitely needed a girl.

They were getting close to Mrs Clotted Cream's place. Mark thought that there was probably no point in entering through the porch, because Mrs Clotted Cream would immediately see from the kitchen window that not three, but four pairs of feet were stomping up the stone steps.

"Wait!" he commanded in a hushed tone, stopping at the edge of the plum orchard. "We need to think about this."

"My tummy's rumbling," complained Pudding, but he stopped obediently.

"We need a way to sneak her into the house. We can't say anything to Mrs Clotted Cream, or she'll make a huge fuss. Macadamia will sleep in my bed."

"What about you?" wondered Annie.

"Me? I'm going to look for... Clementine!" replied Mark, and proudly puffed out his chest. Now he knew what he had to do—yes, he had to find Clementine, who must also be out there, crying with fear in the dark forest.

"I'm going with you!" cried Annie, jumping up and down, her funny little pigtails bouncing with her.

"So am I!" shouted Pudding, afraid as ever of being left alone, but at once he remembered the dark forest, and his heart sank. "So am I," he repeated a little more softly. "But on condition you don't... lose me!"

"OK, we'll try not to lose you! Now climb through this hole."

Mark slid a board in the fence aside and held it back with his knee until Pudding's heels had disappeared into the yard.

"Annie and Macadamia will go in through the window. Pudding will run up the steps, stomping loudly; I'm going to Eddie and Freddie's. Wait here for my instructions. Bye!" said Mark, and he ran off towards the cottage next door.

2.

In which we find out what three
pairs of clean feet are good for

===

"B5!" SAID FREDDIE AND GIGGLED VERY QUIETLY.

"Missed!" replied Eddie, glancing with satisfaction at the sheet of graph paper on which he had cleverly positioned his naval fleet.

"OK then, G9!" Freddie tried again.

"Hit!" said Eddie, alarmed. "My aircraft carrier!"

"You're done for!"

"Never!" said Eddie, marking the ignoble blow to his ship on his grid.

Eddie and Freddie were also staying at the Holiday Hamlet. It was their grandmother's hope that they would "put on some flesh" and "build up". It wasn't entirely clear why "putting on flesh", in other words, getting fatter, was supposed to happen in summer, when you spend your time running about the fields and the woods. Grandma must have known why, but apart from turning a chocolatey shade of brown, Eddie and Freddie hadn't gained any weight at all!

The brothers had made friends with their three young neighbours, and they held cherry-stone-spitting competitions and played Red Indians together. The only thing they didn't join in with was visiting the Frog King, and this was for two reasons:

Firstly, they always ate supper at that time.

Secondly, they really (but really, truly) hated frogs!

"G8, 7 and 6," said Freddie sounding very relieved.

Eddie scrupulously marked the defeat of his aircraft carrier on the graph paper, sticking the tip of his tongue out as he did so. Then he looked up at his brother with a frown.

"Why are you tapping?"

"Me, tapping?" said Freddie in surprise, and pricked up his ears.

TAP. TAP. TAP.

"That's not me! Someone's tapping on the window!"

Freddie gingerly stood up from his chair and grabbed his bow and arrow, ready and waiting, "just in case". He tiptoed towards the window. Suddenly he wheeled round, bow and arrow pointing straight at Eddie's chest.

"What are you doing, you nutcase!" shrieked Eddie, taking cover under the table.

"Just in case you take a peek at my battleships!"

Freddie cautiously poked his head out of the window. Nothing. Darkness. Just the tall pine trees rustling in the distance.

"Shhh... Freddie, it's me, Mark"—he heard a theatrical whisper coming from a clump of burdock below the window.

"Why are you hiding?" Freddie set his bow against the wall and hopped onto the windowsill. It was more comfortable to talk that way. Eddie sat down next to his brother and four thin, sandalled legs swung freely from the raised ground-floor window.

"I had to knock," whispered Mark, poking his head out from under the huge burdock leaves. "Any chance you can come down?"

"What for?" they asked in unison.

"It's a serious matter. It has to remain a secret. The thing is, we've found a little girl..."

"Well I never," muttered Freddie. "She's probably just arrived on holiday."

"You dimwit!" snapped Mark, because he felt terribly uncomfortable crouching in the leaves and he could feel his left calf going numb. "It's the end of the holidays! Who'd be arriving here now? We found her in the forest... she's called Macadamia!"

"Aha," replied Eddie and Freddie in chorus, giving each other a hesitant look.

"We have to go into the forest," whispered Mark, crawling out of the burdock. "There's another little girl out there, called Clementine, and we need to find her..."

"So do we have to go too?" asked Freddie hesitantly, casting a glance at the black forest looming in the distance.

"No, you don't," said Mark quickly. He certainly didn't want anyone else to find Clementine. "We just need three pairs of clean feet..."

"Clean ones?" asked the boys in surprise.

The astonishment that rang out so clearly in both brothers' voices wasn't entirely unfounded! For after a whole day spent chasing about the forest, in the dust, through the marshes and across the fields damp with dew, it was totally impossible to have clean feet. It really was out of the question. If anyone happens to think the Holiday Hamlet was entirely devoid of water for washing your feet in the evenings, they'd be wrong. There was water—Mrs Matthews's deep, cavernous well was full of crystal-clear water. You just had to want it!

But Freddie and Eddie definitely didn't want it. Or rather, they didn't want to wash. In vain Mrs Matthews would fill a huge tub with water, easily big enough to fit six boys as grubby as Eddie and Freddie. But they always found a way to wriggle out of it.

And now here was Mark, wanting clean feet!

"What for?" they chorused, but with less curiosity this time.

"It's all because of Mrs Clotted Cream," said Mark in a hushed tone. "She always checks our feet before we go to sleep!"

Ah yes, that was true. Mrs Clotted Cream, to whose care their parents often entrusted the three children, carried out this task with dignity and a certain degree of... forbearance.

Just before they fell asleep, she would creep into the children's room, turn on the light, and by the dim glow of a bulb suspended from the ceiling check the cleanliness of three pairs of feet, stuck out for this purpose from the end of the iron bedstead. Who exactly was lying in those beds was so obvious to her that she saw no need to give it a second thought.

THEY ALWAYS FOUND
A WAY TO
WRIGGLE OUT OF IT

Of course, matters would be much more serious if she decided to check the state of their ears, for instance! But that had never yet happened.

"How awful!" sighed the brothers, glancing at their blackened heels.

"You need to take our places in the beds," explained Mark, "and when Mrs Clotted Cream comes in—"

"Oh! So we're supposed to sleep there instead of you?" exclaimed Eddie cheerfully.

"Something like that. We're off to the forest right away."

"Aha," they said in unison again, and exchanged glances. "This could be fun," thought Freddie. He had long dreamt of some kind of adventure, which would mean he could go back to school in September with more lasting memories than the ones he had at the moment.

"Maybe this is my chance," thought Eddie at the same time. Just once in his life he desperately wanted to outdo his brother. It was always Freddie this and Freddie that! He was always the chief, the Great Cockroach, while Eddie was the underling, whether he liked it or not.

"So, what do you say?" whispered Mark anxiously.

"All right," they called back from the window, perhaps a touch too loud for such a big secret.

"OK then, listen to me," said Mark—his other calf was going numb now, and he was getting a crick in his neck from constantly craning up at the window. "Two of the beds will be empty. Macadamia will be in the third one—"

"Ah, instead of Annie!" guessed Eddie.

"Yes. And only stick your feet out. Clean feet!" he added sharply. "Otherwise the whole business will go to pot! I'm going home now to prepare the action plan. You've got to climb through the window at nine-thirty on the dot. Mrs Clotted Cream comes in at ten o'clock."

"Hey!" called Freddie, who wanted to know more about who exactly Macadamia and Clementine were. But Mark had disappeared.

The wind, which had suddenly whipped up from nowhere, whistled menacingly and rippled through the dense jasmine bushes. The distant pines, barely visible against the black sky, were bowing their outspread branches to one another.

"I wouldn't go there," Eddie admitted bravely, expecting to be met with approval.

"Oh, I would," said Freddie casually, casting his brother a disdainful look. He turned and jumped down to the floor. Eddie followed him.

"What for?" asked Eddie.

"What do you mean, what for?"

"What would you go there for?"

"To the forest? Well, why should they be the ones to find her? I could seek out that little girl in the forest too! And besides, that kind of deed wins you medals!"

"What sort of medals?" asked Eddie.

"For bravery!"

Eddie sighed deeply. Freddie had a point. And he knew from experience that he would follow his brother into the dark and distant forest. The temptation was stronger than the fear. There was just the question of the feet...

"What can we wash them with?" he asked, remembering that they had thrown the soap into the bushes the day before.

"Maybe with washing powder, or that stuff Mrs Matthews uses to scrub the saucepans..."

"OK, let's go!"

They crept into the hallway. The kitchen door was ajar. Eddie carefully peered through the gap. Not seeing anyone, he slipped inside and grabbed the tin of scouring powder that was standing on the kitchen stove.

"Now let's get outside, quickly!"

Moments later they were duly scrubbing their feet in a bucketful of rainwater, green caterpillars and fallen leaves.

"Up to the knees is enough, right?" bargained Eddie, waving his legs about to dry them quicker.

"Now pay attention," said Freddie, raising a cautionary finger, just as their teacher did at school. "As soon as Mrs Clotted Cream leaves the room, we leap out of the window and run to join in the search..."

"Do you think we'll be quicker than them?"

"Of course! Pudding plods along like a tortoise! They'll be crawling!" sniggered Freddie.

Now that the question of clean feet, which was essentially their hardest problem, had been more or less resolved, there was nothing to stop the boys from very quietly and cautiously stealing their way across the yard to the path that joined the two cottages. It was a narrow, sandy path, which Annie called "Victors' Parade", or "Losers' Alley", depending on the success or failure of a battle. So as they glided down the edge of this path, they were both thinking about the same thing, but in a very different way. Freddie was wondering whether it might not be a good idea to let one of the grown-ups in on the secret. But who? Their parents were, as they say, over the hills and far away... Mrs Matthews? No, out of the question! She'd make an almighty fuss at the mere mention of a night-time expedition! And on the other hand, there was that idea of a medal for bravery. Eddie was definitely afraid. There was no doubt about it. So all the responsibility would fall, as usual, onto his shoulders—Freddie's! Tough. He simply had to lead his two-man team, of which he was both a member and naturally the commander rolled into one. The expedition wasn't going to be easy. It was dark. What's more, they were supposed to stay with that... what was her name again? Oh yes, Macadamia. What a weird name! It sounded like something inedible that grown-ups give you as a snack when they won't let you have cake, so they feed you dry, disgusting nuts. Yuck! But this time it was a little girl. "She shouldn't be left on her own again," thought Freddie. "But then she will be staying indoors. That's something. And in a warm bed! We need to find out a bit more from her about the other girl, Clementine, who's lost in the forest... Yes. That'll give us a better chance of pinpointing where exactly she disappeared. Then we'll be able to find her much more quickly than the others. We absolutely must get the better of them and finally proclaim ourselves the great and unrivalled victors of the holiday!"

Eddie meanwhile was wondering what that poor little girl was doing all alone in the dreadful forest. "What if someone lost me, for instance?" he thought. "Of course, no one could lose me, I'm already big—but what if? What would I do then? I'd probably be afraid! I definitely would!"

The boys quickened their pace.

"What time do you think it is?" asked Freddie.

Eddie looked up at the stars.

"If the sun were up I bet I could tell you. But it's too dark now!"

"Too bad," said Freddie, grappling with the same loose fence board on the orchard side.

They fought their way through the raspberry bushes. Freddie made a brief stop under a plum tree to pick two big plums.

"Here, but hurry up!" he said, handing Eddie a plum.

"'Urryup?" burbled Eddie with his mouth full. He had to stop for a moment to dig out a handkerchief from the depths of his pocket. He hurriedly wiped off the juice that was running down his chin and galloped after Freddie.

The others were already waiting. They were lurking under the window, using sign language to show that the coast was clear.

"Just don't scare her!" whispered Annie to Eddie. "She cries about anything at all!" And she was gone.

"It's as if she dissolved into thin air!" thought Eddie, but he had no chance to ponder this idea, because Freddie was beckoning to him.

They hopped over the windowsill and tiptoed up to the bed, where the rather frightened Macadamia was sitting.

"Hi," said Freddie, shifting from foot to foot. He felt very awkward.

It was an entirely natural feeling, because Freddie and Eddie didn't have a sister and had nothing to do with girls. Except for Annie—that was completely different. Firstly, she was Mark and Pudding's sister, and they counted as friends, and secondly, she was just so different! She never snivelled, and she was brilliant at moving stealthily!

"Hi," repeated Eddie and sat down on the edge of the bed.

"Do you know what you're meant to do?" asked Freddie.

"Yes," whispered Macadamia, and immediately hid under the quilt, sticking her little bare feet through the bars at the end of the bed.

"Great! Eddie, get under the quilt, quick."

They were in the beds in a flash. And just in time, because seconds later they heard Mrs Clotted Cream saying goodbye to a busybody friend of hers on the doorstep.

Their hearts beating fast, all three children lay waiting for Mrs Clotted Cream to switch on the light. They were so terribly afraid that when the moment actually came it escaped their notice.

"Are you asleep, kiddies?" Mrs Clotted Cream's voice rumbled around the room exactly like thunder rolling across the sky. "Feet all clean? Good! Looks like there's a storm brewing, doesn't it?"

And the light went out. They were safe! Freddie waited a moment, then signalled to Eddie. Macadamia stuck her head out from under the quilt and stared at the boys with curiosity.

"Are you going too?"

"Of course! Just tell us one thing—what's this... Clementine wearing?"

"Wearing?" Macadamia gaped in surprise.

"Yeah, what colour?"

"Grey, but—"

"Oh drat! Looking for grey in this darkness!" said Freddie anxiously.

"But she has a red headscarf. The only colour she likes is red! Unless she's lost it again. She's always losing her headscarves!" sobbed Macadamia.

"Shh, don't cry! We'll definitely find her."

"And bring her back here!"

It occurred to Eddie that nothing was quite so certain, but just then Freddie tugged at his trouser leg. They waved to the little girl, and in a single bound they landed in the orchard.

The wind was whistling. A strange, silvery-grey cloud was approaching from the direction of the town. Eddie glanced at the sky and remembered how scared he was of storms, but was too ashamed to tell his brother. Freddie meanwhile was thinking exactly the same thing. They both sighed quietly and strode down the path, barely visible in the darkness.

3.

In which we find out what happens
when you eavesdrop on other
people's telephone conversations

===

THE BANDITS ARE GETTING CLOSER. TEDDY STRIDES
along, as fast as he can. If he can just reach that house,
the one looming on the horizon... The bandits are speed-
ing up too. They're right on his heels. The scariest one
of all is so close that Teddy can feel his rapid breathing
on the back of his neck.

THE BANDITS ARE
GETTING CLOSER

RRRRING! RRRRRING!

What's that? A car horn? Where's the house? Where have the bandits gone?

RRRRING!

Teddy sat up in bed with a start. So that was just a dream? What a terrible nightmare! With eyes wide open, he stared at the barely visible shape of the window. It was dark, the dead of night.

RRRING!!

The insistent noise kept drilling into his brain. The telephone! In Dad's office! As usual, Dad couldn't hear it!

Teddy leapt out of bed and was already sprinting for the door when he heard the characteristic patter of Dad's slippers coming from the next room. He pushed the door ajar and poked his tousled head through the gap.

"Hello? Yes! This is Sergeant Beeper. What's happened? What? I can't hear anything!"

Teddy shivered, suddenly feeling a cold draught on his bare feet. The wind had picked up and was hammering on the shutters. "Maybe there's a storm brewing?" he thought, shifting from foot to foot. "Who's calling in the middle of the night? Maybe something exciting has happened!"

"Helloo?" called Sergeant Beeper, anxiously tapping on the telephone cradle. "Who's lost? A child? What child? Whose? I can't hear you..."

Well! This had never happened before. Teddy tiptoed back to his bed and put on his shabby old slippers. He wrapped a blanket around his shoulders and returned to his post by the door. This could be interesting. A child! Where could a child have got lost? And whose child? He peeked through the gap in the door and saw his father blowing fitfully into the well-used telephone receiver. Dad was in his pyjamas. He looked so funny! Nothing like a police sergeant. Dad in his uniform—now that was a different story.

Teddy was, of course, incredibly proud of his dad the policeman, but deep down he couldn't help thinking that in his everyday working methods Dad didn't seem much like a detective!

After all, the village police station in St Jude's was a far cry from the splendid study of the famous detective, Sherlock Holmes, whose adventures Teddy had watched on television. Dad refused to smoke the pipe that Teddy had bought him for his birthday with the money he'd saved up specially. But the pipe was nothing compared with the fact that Dad had no idea how to play the violin!

Meanwhile, the phone was still making intermittent strange noises, and although Dad was pressing the receiver to his ear harder and harder he still couldn't hear a thing—not a squeak—beyond the crackling noise coming out of it.

"Hello!! So what's this about a child? Oh, a little girl! She went where? Into the forest?"

Into the forest! Teddy was so surprised he sank to the floor. A little girl had gone into the forest on her own at night! But why? Wasn't she afraid? That was odd. On the whole, little girls weren't known to move about in the dark by themselves from one room to another, let alone into the woods!

"Who did you say she was following? I can't hear you! Clementine? And who is that? Hellooo? Helloo!"

And they were cut off. The conversation was interrupted as suddenly as if someone had sliced through the cable with a knife. Sergeant Beeper blew into the receiver a few more times, but to no avail. The phone remained silent. The sergeant frowned and muttered something under his breath that Teddy couldn't hear from that distance. And probably a good thing too, because the slings and arrows being fired from Dad's lips at telephones and modern technology in general, and the age of progress in particular, were most unsuitable for Teddy's still youthful ears.

"It's an outrage! What sort of a report is that?" said the sergeant angrily.

Teddy opened the door wider and freed himself from the blanket. He couldn't stop wondering what an unknown girl could be doing in the forest.

"Dad," he began hesitantly. "She will be OK, won't she?"

"Who? Who are you talking about? And what are you doing up at this time of night anyway?"

Not even Teddy knew how to answer that. He was perfectly well aware that eavesdropping on other people's telephone conversations, and particularly Dad's work calls, was strictly forbidden.

"Well, the phone rang..."

"It did indeed! But I couldn't understand a thing!" said the sergeant forlornly, sitting down on his chair.

"Apparently a little girl has got lost, so I'll have to go and look for her..."

"But how are you going to do that? In the forest, at night?"

That was a question Sergeant Beeper couldn't answer.

Nor did he know the real intention behind that seemingly innocent question.

The fact is, Teddy had longed to take part in a Major Operation for years. He had, of course, borrowed the term "Major Operation" from a crime novel he'd read, and to his mind it involved an extraordinary experience—and he wanted to do it as soon as possible, because the end of the holidays was inevitably drawing near, and with it any chance of a big adventure. Obviously, the Major Operation couldn't be just the usual sort of holiday escapade, because the very word "operation" was so important and serious that it demanded at least an entire police squadron, some machine guns and a pack of well-trained dogs.

Or at least one dog!

But where could he find a machine gun? And that many policemen? Apart from Sergeant Beeper, the police station in St Jude's only had Constable Podger, who, though this might seem funny, was not in the least bit fat. On the contrary, he was as long and thin as a rake. What about the dogs, then? No problem! Teddy had his own, beloved Pickles, with whom he shared all his happiest and saddest moments, and quite often his soup bowl as well.

Pickles was a large, black-and-tan German shepherd, with a friendly expression and an extremely sunny temperament. Dad liked to make fun of Pickles's plainly not entirely pedigree descent, but this had no bearing on the mutual love between boy and dog. So of all the items required for a Major Operation, the only one Teddy had was a dog. And not the kind of obedient, well-trained dog the situation demanded. But in any case, there was no sign of an operation yet, not even a very minor one!

"Dad, are you going to look for... what's her name?..."

"Of course! I'll send Constable Podger to police headquarters in town right away. He can explain that the telephone report was incomprehensible, and that the cable must have broken... Perhaps we can organize a joint search... But quick march! Off to bed with you!"

Teddy was full of energy now and had absolutely no desire to go to bed. "On the contrary," he thought. "Maybe I should take some action of my own." But what? The little girl was probably sitting under a tree, or worse still wandering about in the dense undergrowth. The forest was big, to be sure, and the chances of finding her at night were small. That kind of operation worked better during the day. But by daybreak the whole thing would be over! Any minute now Dad would start dealing with it, along with the police, and his opportunity would be lost! The police had dogs, cars and all their so-called "equipment". Dad would call for backup from town and then... so long, Major Operation. So he'd have to take independent action, and do so before Constable Podger reached town.

Teddy stole another glance at his father, who was drumming his fingers on the table. The phone was silent.

"Teddy, just go back to bed and don't be a nuisance—I have to get dressed!"

Teddy nodded. This was just what he'd been waiting for. As an operation complete with machine guns was out of the question, he, Teddy Beeper, would have to carry out a solo mission. But what would it be called? It had to have a name, of course—a code name, as the police would say. Teddy sat on the bed and put his head in his hands to think. It's very hard to come up with something off the cuff! Maybe "Operation Clementine"? As well as that, he'd have to leave Dad a letter, so he stood up and quietly padded over to the table. He tore a page from a notebook, though that was something he never did, and started to write in red pencil:

DEAR DAD, I HEREBY REPORT THAT OPERATION 'CLEMENTINE' HAS BEGUN. I AM GOING WITH PICKLES HE HAS A NOSE LIKE AT SKOTLANDYARD. IN CASE OF NOTHING, SEND CANINE REINFORCEMENTS. BYE, TEDDY.

Teddy looked at the piece of paper, read it through again and smiled with satisfaction. That was good information! Dad always said that the best reports were brief and to the point. And this had everything it needed. He considered the words "in case of nothing" for a while, then shrugged. It was obvious what it meant. He went over to the window and looked up at the sky. It was definitely about to rain. "Just as long as there isn't a storm! I'll take a compass and Pickles. That should be enough. And a torch. You can't get by at night without a torch. If they've called Dad," reasoned Teddy, "the girl must be lost in our forest. But how do they know about it in town? Something doesn't make sense. The town is thirty kilometres from St Jude's! No, she can't have wandered all the way from town. That's out of the question. Dad's right that that piece of information has to be checked. Never mind. We'll give it a try! Maybe she's somewhere nearby?" He had to begin by taking the path near the four huge oak trees, the one he knew so well. He knew almost every tree and every bush around here. Either way, it was time to set off. Before they managed to fix the phone line and before Dad started to take action.

"Teddy, are you asleep?" he heard his dad ask.

He leapt into bed and pulled the quilt up to his ears.

"Teddy, I'm going to see Constable Podger. The phone still isn't working."

"OK, Dad," he replied, trembling with fear that Dad would notice the letter on the table. But nothing happened. Dad didn't even switch on the light, and closed the door behind him.

Teddy waited a moment and then jumped out of bed. He dressed quickly and, taking care not to make a noise, clambered onto the windowsill. From there it was just one leap into the garden. Pickles gave a joyful yelp in his kennel. Teddy stroked his head affectionately.

"Come on, boy! We're going on a Major Operation!"

He checked that his torch and his compass were working properly.

The dog was wagging his tail and jumping up and down. He was clearly very pleased about this unexpected walk.

"Quiet, shhhh..." whispered Teddy, holding Pickles's mouth shut with his hand. "Don't bark, it's not allowed!"

He opened the little wooden gate and quietly tiptoed over to the path. He had to be very careful now. The path to the forest ran right past Constable Podger's house. And as Dad had just gone over there... running into him by accident was a real risk. It had to be avoided at all costs!

Teddy sneaked along the fence with Pickles silently running after him. The dog's ears were pricked up and alert to the faintest rustle.

And so they reached the green gate that led into Constable Podger's garden. Suddenly, Pickles froze and growled softly. Teddy flung himself against the thick trunk of an apple tree.

"You must go to town immediately," came the sergeant's voice out of the darkness.

"In the jeep, Sergeant?"

"No, the motorbike will do."

"I'll be off right away!"

"Report to the police chief there, find out exactly what has happened, and come back immediately. The motorbike is in my shed. I'll give you a report too."

"Yes, sir!" cried Constable Podger in an official-sounding voice.

The sergeant came down the terribly creaky wooden steps from the porch, and opened the green gate. Teddy clung ever more closely to the tree trunk. He was holding

Pickles's muzzle as tightly shut as he could, terrified that the dog would run up to Dad, who mustn't catch sight of him, of course.

Without suspecting a thing, the sergeant walked past a step away from the dog's tail. Deep in thought, his head bowed, he made for home. Teddy waited a while longer, patted the dog, and headed off down the path.

* * * *

It was as dark as a coal mine, and a heavy storm was brewing too. It soon grew even darker, and a silver cloud now covered the whole sky. Gusts of wind kept blowing, battering the limbs of the trees. It looked extremely miserable. It was impossible to believe that this was the same green and sunny wood where all the children from the Holiday Hamlet played their most fabulous games!

For that matter, Pudding wasn't looking too jolly either. He was trailing along behind Annie, glowering at the dark wall of trees. Mark, on the other hand, was marching along quite bravely, wondering whether, instead of walking in single file, it might not be better to enter the forest spread out in formation, like soldiers on a battlefield. Or like freedom fighters. But would the others agree to it? They could hoot to each other from time to time. But no, they wouldn't want to split up for anything in the world. Pudding would be the first to complain, of course. And worse yet, he would start howling. And there was nothing worse on this planet than the sound of Pudding howling. Besides, the little girl couldn't be far off. Macadamia had pointed them in the right direction. She must be somewhere in the vicinity of the Frog King's empire. Or in any case, not much further away.

"Perhaps we should take him home after all?" asked Annie, taking Pudding by the hand.

"No! I won't go! I want to come with you!"

"Don't yell," said Mark calmly. "We don't have time to go back. We can only hope you don't start snivelling!"

"I won't," said Pudding in a sugary tone.

"It's a good thing we left Eddie and Freddie behind. They can look after Macadamia," said Mark, feeling the full weight of responsibility for the little girl's safety.

* * * *

Well, how was he to know that Eddie and Freddie had already set off after them, following the same path? Their task was even harder. They had to stay hidden—from Mark's group, of course. They had to avoid bumping into any one of them at all costs. Freddie was convinced that finding Clementine was the most important task that had come their way in the whole of that year's holiday. Freddie was determined to find the girl before Mark did.

Somehow, the fact that it was very easy for the children to get lost themselves in such a big forest simply hadn't crossed any of their minds. Freddie's ambition wouldn't allow for any fear, while Mark was only thinking about the mysterious stranger, who might be wandering about behind this bush or maybe that one. Of course, the distance between Mark's group and Freddie and Eddie was quite big, because the brothers had set out at least half an hour later, if not longer...

* * * *

But a sixth person knew the secret and was in the forest too! Teddy had absolutely no idea that anyone else had already gone into the forest for the same purpose as he had. How could he have known that? Teddy had never even met the other children. By a strange chance, living at the other end of the village, he had never had the opportunity of encountering them. He played with other friends who had come to the village on holiday too, but who to his great regret had already gone home.

So it was that Teddy was the last to leave home, and as he and Pickles were walking down the path, the five other detectives had already been in the forest for quite some time.

BUT A SIXTH PERSON KNEW THE SECRET AND WAS IN THE FOREST TOO!

4.

In which we find out who is driven up
the wall by his red car's sneezes

===

MR IGNATIUS PROSSER—A REPORTER FOR A NATIONAL
newspaper who filled several pages a day with the most
sensational news—was feeling tired. The tiredness was
making his life a real misery, because it had set in while
Mr Prosser was sitting behind the wheel of his little
red car, which had stopped in the middle of the road.
Let's just add that it was an unfamiliar road, because
the journey that the reporter had undertaken was the
sort of journey that takes you... into the unknown.
Equally unknown was the origin of the strange sneeze-
like noises that were coming from under the bonnet.

None of this would have been quite so upsetting, if
not for that fact that Mr Prosser was separated from

the nearest town by about thirty kilometres of bumpy road, which the maps of the region had grandly labelled a "highway".

The sneezing was preventing him from calmly reviewing the situation. It sounded as if there were six cats with catarrh inside the engine.

Mr Prosser, who was quite short-tempered, should have been seething with rage over the sneezing car by now, but he was too tired for that.

The little red car—a never-ending source of worry and bother—was supposed to be taking him for a well-deserved break at a forester's lodge where a friend of his was staying—a painter called Phosphorus Twisk.

But in Mr Prosser's present situation, the idea of a nice rest at Mr Twisk's forester's lodge was becoming more remote with every passing minute.

"What am I to do?" he wondered, tapping the end of his umbrella against the complicated tangle of metal that filled the space underneath the bonnet.

"Maybe the problem's here? Or maybe it's somewhere else entirely?"

Mr Prosser sighed heavily and wiped the sweat from

his brow. He cast a glance at the sky and his heart sank. It was going to rain! Perhaps there was even a storm brewing! That would be worst of all. The red open-top car offered no protection—Mr Prosser was entirely bereft of what is commonly known as a roof over one's head.

The road led through fields and young copses, which couldn't provide any shelter from the imminent rain. Mr Prosser took a large road map out of the glove compartment and unfolded it on his knees. He switched on his torch, and with the tip of a pencil he traced the lines representing a tangled network of roads.

"I'm here," he said to himself, and sighed again. Unfortunately, the spot where he was sitting was still very far from the forester's lodge, which was right at the heart of the forest.

And the car was still sneezing.

"He's probably tucking into scrambled eggs," thought Mr Prosser, imagining his painter friend. "Maybe he's even used five eggs." That was too much to bear! He could forgive just about anything, but the idea that right then and there Phosphorus Twisk was tucking into scrambled eggs...

"No!" shouted Mr Prosser, leaping to his feet. "That I refuse to accept!"

As though in response to his desperate outburst, a sudden flash lit up the sky and a peal of thunder rumbled in the distance.

"A storm!" moaned Mr Prosser, and began rapping twice as hard on the coils of pipes and other metal parts making up the engine.

"Achoo! Achoo!" replied the car.

Mr Prosser spun round on his own axis and kicked the bumper with all his might. And a miracle happened! The engine sneezed, snorted and roared with the full force of its mechanical horsepower.

BOOOOOM!

The rumble of thunder hadn't yet died away before another flash of lightning cut the black sky in two. Mr Prosser leapt into the driver's seat and put his foot on the accelerator, and instantly the car shot forwards.

BABOOOOOOM!

5.

In which someone gets lost in the forest, but as there's a storm, that doesn't surprise anyone

==

BABOOOOM!!

A GIGANTIC GREEN BOLT OF LIGHTNING CUT RIGHT across the sky, merging with a peal of thunder into one terrifying "rumbleflash". All of a sudden the pitch-black forest was lit up as bright as day.

"Help!" screamed Pudding and raced headlong as fast as his legs could carry him.

"Stop!" shouted Annie and Mark in chorus, afraid of losing him in the forest.

But Pudding's reaction was hardly surprising! The same lightning bolt had also terrified Mr Prosser, who was an adult, after all.

"I'm ssscared!" Pudding stammered out his usual refrain.

It had gone very dark again, and the wind was yanking at their hair and clothes, while strewing the ground with snapped-off twigs and leaves.

"At least it's not raining," said Annie, stopping on the path. "Maybe the storm will pass us by."

By now they had been walking for quite a time, keenly looking to either side and shaking the nearest bushes. Even Mark felt that any moment now they would end up on the other side of the forest. They had long since passed the boundary line, marked by three silver spruces standing in file like lead soldiers, beyond which they never ventured further into the forest. Not even during the day. Of course, they had never been in the forest at night before.

Annie took Pudding by the hand and dragged him after her.

"Is he still trembling?" asked Mark, reaching out a hand ahead of him to push aside some withered branches that were hanging down to the path.

"I don't know if he's trembling, but we haven't lost him yet," replied Annie, pushing her little brother in front of her.

"It's not out of fear..." said Pudding. "It's just—"

"Watch out!" shouted Mark suddenly, but... it was too late.

The only thing Annie and Pudding were aware of was a rattling noise, and then the thud of a falling body.

"Heeelp..." came the sound of Mark's voice, but strangely distant and muffled.

BOOOOOM!!!!

There was such a sudden clap of thunder, so totally without warning, that Pudding tore himself free of

BUT...
IT WAS
TOO LATE

Annie's grasp in terror and leapt headlong into the darkness.

"Pudding! Mark! Where are you? Answer me!" shouted Annie, turning helplessly on the spot. Now she was afraid too. It was dreadful. It was as though the forest had come alive, and suddenly it seemed full of rustles, sighs and moans. Now and then little yellow dots flashed in the brushwood, fireflies perhaps, or maybe someone's eyes!

"Mark! Say something!" she screamed, shouting over the rising roar of the wind. All she heard in response was something thrashing about and some muffled groaning.

Here's what had happened to Mark: straying off the path, he had suddenly tripped on a protruding root, fallen over and slipped down a slope into a deep pit full of conifer needles and prickly pine cones.

"I wonder if this is a den of some kind?" he thought, when he finally managed to recover a bit.

In the flash of another lightning bolt, he saw the high edge of the pit and... to his horror, a dark shape falling straight on top of him.

"A bear!" he thought, as he felt a huge weight come crashing down on his head and chest.

Quick as blinking, he let fly with his feet and kicked the enemy with all his might.

"Owww!" howled Pudding in pain and terror, because in fact it was him, scared out of his skin.

"Is that you?" asked Mark, coming to his senses.

"Who else could it be?" burbled Pudding, rubbing his aching bottom. "Who did you think it was? An elephant?"

"I thought it was a bear. Where's Annie?"

"How should I know? There was a sudden flash and then SOMETHING threw me up in the air and dropped me onto your head," mumbled Pudding, trying to find a more comfortable place to sit.

"Annie! Hey! Annieee!" shouted Mark. "Now we're sure to get lost!" he grumbled when he couldn't hear an answer. Mark felt responsible for the fate of his siblings. After all, he was the mainspring, the driving force behind the whole expedition.

"I think she must be sitting in a hole as well," said Pudding, squeezing his eyes shut because the sky above the edge of the pit had gone strangely green and blue again.

"Annie?"

"No, the little girl we're looking for!"

"You know what," said Mark in the confidential tone he used only in the most dangerous situations, "I'm not at all sure we're ever going to find her!"

"What? What do you mean?" Pudding instantly began to blubber, because it had just occurred to him that here he was with Mark, while poor little Clementine was somewhere out there all by herself.

On top of that, the thought of their own comfortable beds, and the warm blankets under which Eddie and Freddie were now dozing, was so painful that poor Pudding began to whimper.

As for Mark, incredible as it may seem, he was thinking wistfully about the glass of warm milk that he always refused, even at breakfast time.

Just at that moment, torrential rain came lashing down. It happened so quickly and with so little warning that Mark leapt up as if scalded, hitting his head on a hard protrusion. He reached upwards, and to his great surprise felt something like a roof above him, made up of knotted roots and dry branches.

"Pudding, come here!" he shouted.

Soaking wet and utterly miserable, his little brother squatted beside him.

"It cccould be a lion's dden!" he stammered, trembling from head to toe.

"It could indeed!" said Mark, laughing. "But I think the lion's gone out for a walk right now..."

"You're always laughing at me, but I'm soaking wet!" Pudding was shivering, more from fear than from cold.

"Think of Clementine! She's been wandering about the forest for ages and she's on her own..."

"What about Annie? She's on her own too, and she's—"

BOOMMM! BOOOOMM!

Pudding shuddered and glued himself to Mark. It was raining cats and dogs, as they say. Streams of water were lashing the tops of the trees, showering against the leaves and falling like hail onto the dense forest undergrowth. After each bolt of lightning it grew even darker and more terrible. The wind was tearing at the branches and howling like a pack of wolves.

"I want Annieee!" stammered Pudding, clinging ever more tightly to Mark's back.

"Don't blubber, old chap," said Mark, giving him a friendly poke in the ribs. "I think we're going to be looking for two girls now rather than just one."

"Don't you think Annie's looking for us now?" asked Pudding. He was very worried about his sister.

Of course, there was another reason for worrying about Annie. Apart from feeling real concern about the girls' fate, Pudding was trying to drown out his own fear. As everyone knows, if during a storm you think very, very hard about something completely different, the storm seems to grow smaller and the fear isn't quite as powerful.

They had no idea how long they'd been sitting in that hole, which though dry was very, if not extremely, uncomfortable.

"This is a one-person hole," said Mark, whose calves were going numb again.

"You're not going to drive me out of here, are you?" asked Pudding in a very shrill tone.

"No way!" replied Mark, clenching his teeth because a hundred thousand frenzied ants were running around his calf by now. Pins and needles always feels like ants are crawling about on you.

The rain seemed to be letting up, but flashes of lightning were still illuminating the edge of their hideaway, and peals of thunder came roaring one after another. The whole forest was rumbling and crackling like kindling burning on an open fire.

"Will it last much longer?" asked Pudding, squeezing his eyes shut so tightly they hurt.

"As long as it doesn't flood our..." began Mark, and suddenly stopped.

"Flood our what?" asked Pudding nervously. Mark had frozen on the spot and was staring into the darkness with wide-open eyes.

"Well, why don't you answer?" said Pudding, tugging at his sleeve.

"Look! Look!" stammered Mark, retreating into the depths of the pit. There, at the edge of it, in the pitch darkness a pair of green eyes were shining.

* * * *

For a while, Annie stood on the spot, wondering what to do. She was afraid to take a single step. She had no idea where Mark and Pudding had gone all of a sudden! Gusts of wind were bending the branches of the nearest tree, making them turn semicircles in the air like swirling green broomsticks.

Suddenly cold conifer needles brushed against her cheek.

"Aaaargh!" she screamed and leapt backwards in a single bound. That saved her from falling into the same hole that had already swallowed Mark and Pudding. But Annie didn't know that. What was worse, she had completely lost her sense of direction. She didn't know which way to run so, without realizing what she was doing, she fled back down the same path they had taken to get there. She raced along it at breakneck speed as the lightning flared, illuminating the path in a clear, black line.

BOOOOM!

Another thunderbolt struck the ground, and with it came a torrential downpour. "What should I do? Where can I hide? During a thunderstorm you mustn't stand under a tree"—her father's words flashed through her mind. But where else could you stand during a thunderstorm in a very dense forest?

She came to a fork in the path. On the right she could see some tangled bushes. Beyond them was a glade. "I'll crawl in there," she thought, "under those branches." She had no idea how long she spent in that rather uncomfortable position. Once the forest had quietened down, and the distant flashes were only faintly lighting up the pitch darkness, Annie caught sight of a huge tree growing a few metres to the left of the path. Its trunk was very thick, and its spreading boughs were swaying in the wind. Against the backdrop of the black sky, its dense crown looked silvery white. Two metres above the ground the hefty trunk seemed to have cracked open, forming a large hole.

"A hollow!" whispered the girl.

Climbing onto the first branch, which hung low to the ground, posed no great difficulty. They had conquered bigger trees than this one over the summer! Annie grabbed the next branch with her left hand and pulled herself up. She dangled there for a moment, trying to find a support for her right foot. There it was! A small chip of bark, protruding from the trunk.

CRAASSH!

As the ground and the tree suddenly went spinning around her, she landed with a thud on the wet moss. She leapt to her feet immediately, rubbing her sore spot.

"I'm going to have a bruise," she muttered, and keenly started to climb the tree again—more carefully this time.

Raindrops falling from the wet leaves trickled down her neck in a cold stream.

"Brr!" she shivered, and tightly holding on to the slippery branches, she finally reached the edge of the hollow she'd been aiming for. "What if there's an animal living inside?" she suddenly thought, balancing on one leg. She grabbed a protruding twig, which snapped with a dry crack. Leaning out as far as she could, she tossed the twig into the hollow.

In the greenish flash that briefly lit up the hollow, all she saw were a few of last year's old acorns and a soft layer of woodchips. Finders keepers! Taking care not to fall, Annie knelt on the rim of the hollow, and then slipped confidently inside. She crouched on the soft dust that padded the bottom and sighed deeply. She felt safe. Through the oval opening she could see trees and bushes being lashed by the wind. The forest shook and creaked.

"Just like an old wardrobe," she thought, settling down more comfortably. She wasn't afraid any more. The hollow—big and spacious, smelling of acorns and that special aroma of old wood—made a wonderful shelter.

"But where are the boys? I hope nothing's happened to them! Pudding's a trooper, but he might catch a chill and end up with the flu. How on earth did he disappear before my very eyes?" Annie was extremely worried, because frankly, her little brother was her special favourite. Her only comfort was the thought

that Mark and Pudding were probably together. And what about that poor little Clementine?

Meanwhile, as often happens in summer, the storm that had been sudden and ferocious in the first instance, was now just rain falling in big, warm drops. The lightning flashes were distant and rare, and the rumbles of thunder were more like the growling of an angry cat.

Annie leant against the wall of the hollow and closed her eyes. She suddenly felt very sleepy. What time could it be? It was still the middle of the night, and she'd probably have to stay there until dawn, and then go in search of Mark, Pudding and poor little Clementine. Perhaps Mark had already found her? What a shame! Annie had so badly wanted to be there when they finally found her. She imagined the three of them (because of course the boys were bound to turn up!) bringing the rescued child back to the village. Mum and Dad would be proud of their children for being so brave and daring, proud of them in general...

Poor Annie was so sleepy and tired out by her chase through the darkness and the rain that her thoughts flowed unusually idly. As the forest fell silent around her, the only sound to be heard was the wind whistling overhead from time to time, making the thick old oak tree creak gently. It was as if it were talking to the other trees in its ancient voice about the recent storm.

Or maybe that was just how it felt to Annie, as she sat with her eyes closed, listening in on those mysterious murmurs?

6.

In which Freddie and Eddie have a
terrible time and fall into a trap

==

FREDDIE AND EDDIE WERE MARCHING BRISKLY
ahead. Now that they no longer had to worry about
the cleanliness of their feet, they were happily plung-
ing them into the soft layer of fine sand that covered
the path. The forest that stood like a black wall right
behind the barns suddenly didn't seem so terrible any
more. Perhaps it was the joy of having an adventure
that did it, or perhaps the night outside was simply
not as black as it looked when you saw it through the
bedroom window.

They passed the border marked by the three spruces
in silence, and probably without even realizing that
they had crossed into unfamiliar territory.

"Why are you so quiet?"

Freddie didn't reply. He was staring into the darkness that lay like a soft shroud over the forest, making it impossible to discern the contours of the individual trees.

"Freddie, I'm talking to you!"

"I hear you! Don't shout like an idiot!" he hissed in reply. "Are you scared or something?"

"As if!" protested Eddie, who was actually finding his brother's stubborn silence quite unbearable. And just at that moment he suddenly began to feel scared. He felt cold, but at the same time his shirt was sticking to his sweaty back. He was longing to hold his brother's hand. He was afraid that Freddie might suddenly disappear into the darkness and leave him in the clutches of the night and the wind.

"Do you hear that?" he said, grabbing Freddie by the arm. "Something's wailing!"

"Nothing's wailing! It's just the wind," said Freddie angrily, freeing his arm from Eddie's grip. "How ghastly! Eddie's such a coward!" he thought to himself, brushing some thorny branches aside with his hand. "Watch out, don't scratch yourself," he muttered, because he suddenly felt sorry for his brother. "Don't worry, we'll find her right away! I'm sure she'll be crying very loud just like girls always do. We'll hear her and..."

BOOOOOM!!!

"Oh no! Thunder and lightning!" moaned Eddie, squatting on the path.

"You're right, it's a storm," said Freddie. "Now we won't hear anything, not even if she's crying really loud!"

"You see," mumbled Eddie, his eyes tightly closed. "And you said we'd find her in an instant!"

"So what? You can go home if you want!" shouted Freddie over the noise of the wind.

"I dddon't know if I want anything at all," stammered Eddie, pressing his fists to his eyes to avoid seeing the menacing flashes of lightning.

"Oh, come on! Let's keep going!" commanded Freddie firmly. Then he took Eddie's hand and pulled him after him.

Over their heads the storm and the forest were whistling and creaking, united in a single ominous, harsh and hostile din.

"Freddie! Let's find shelter somewhere! It's force twelve on the Beaufort scale!"

"So what?"

"Do you know how much that is? That's when the wind speed is a hundred and thirty kilometres an hour!"

"That's nothing, a racing car goes faster than that!" shouted back Freddie in a moment of quiet.

"A fat lot you know about it!" yelled Eddie, hugging a thick tree trunk for balance.

"Let's get away from here! This pine tree's creaking suspiciously!" shouted Freddie.

Eddie had a hard time ungluing himself from the tree. Left without protection, he stumbled forwards, pushed by a sudden gust of wind. The rain was getting into his eyes and trickling down his back and his trouser legs in a cold, thin stream.

"I'm soaked to the skin!" he said, wiping his face. "Listen, where are we actually going?"

"To the teddy bears' picnic!" Freddie shouted back furiously. "You know we have to find Clementine in order to win that medal!"

"I don't think I even want a medal," muttered Eddie, wrapping his arms around the tree trunk again. "And I'm not budging an inch! Over there," he said, pointing towards the undergrowth, "it's definitely even worse!"

At that moment they both suddenly froze. Over the moaning of the gale and the booming of the thunder they could hear another, infinitely more menacing noise.

"Wolves!" screamed Eddie.

"Quick, up this tree!" Freddie reached out wildly for the outspread branches of a thick beech tree.

Now they could clearly hear some kind of hulking body forcing its way through the undergrowth.

Paralysed by fear, Eddie was unable to move.

"Eddie! Come here, to me!" yelled Freddie, sitting on the lowest branch.

"I ccccan't," wailed Eddie, but at the same moment in a brief flash of light he saw a huge prehistoric creature emerging from behind a nearby spruce. "Heeelp!! Aaargh!" he screamed, and in a single leap found himself next to Freddie, taking no notice of the sharp branches inflicting cuts on his thighs.

Pitch darkness had set in again. It seemed to the boys that the only sound to be heard throughout the forest was the thumping of their terrified hearts, about to burst out of their chests.

The forest had fallen silent. Just now and then a kind of tremor shot through the trees, and a thick hail of raindrops fell from the rustling beech leaves. In the roar of the receding storm both boys suddenly heard a low whistle in the distance.

"Did you hear that? Somebody whistled!"

"It's probably Mark," said Eddie, doing his best to find a slightly more comfortable position on the branch.

"Did you see that animal too?"

Eddie didn't reply.

"I'm asking because now I think maybe I just imagined it," said Freddie, in a tone that was the very negation of fear, although his heart was pounding hard.

"I dddon't know," replied Eddie.

"Maybe it's still somewhere near here."

A distant lightning bolt lit up the dense darkness for a moment.

"No, I think it's gone," replied Eddie. "Maybe it was never there at all," he said, praying inside for his brother to confirm this sudden and most unusual hypothesis. It would be much easier to climb down from the tree if they believed there was nothing at the bottom of it.

"I don't think it was," said Freddie hesitantly, because what he thought he had seen was very unlikely.

"Since it wasn't, maybe we should get down... although... maybe we should stay here a bit longer... just in case," said Eddie, attentively picking up every suspicious rustling noise.

"We can do that," agreed Freddie benignly, shuddering violently as a delayed drop of water suddenly landed on the nape of his neck and ran down his back in a cold trickle.

As Eddie let out a deep sigh his teeth began to chatter of their own accord. "It's probably the cold," he thought, and, as if fate were trying to spite him, he suddenly felt awfully hot.

They were sitting on a thick branch with rough, pale-grey bark. A dense crown of bizarrely plaited branches spread out above their heads. Lit up from time to time by the blue glow of the distant lightning bolts, the oval shape of the beech leaves stood out sharply in the darkness.

"It's pretty cool here actually," said Freddie, tucking his feet under him, "don't you think?"

"Yes," replied Eddie uncertainly, thinking fondly of his comfortable bed.

"I wonder where they are now?" said Freddie, shuffling closer to his brother.

The branch creaked dangerously.

"Yes, indeed," said Eddie glumly, as an image of Annie's thin pigtails flashed before his eyes. "I wonder, do you think she was really scared?"

"Who? Clementine?"

"No, I was thinking of Annie," admitted Eddie, silently grateful for the surrounding darkness, in which Freddie couldn't see the blush filling his cheeks.

"Listen," said Freddie anxiously. "Do you think Mark could have found Clementine by now?"

"No, I don't think so. Not in such a bad storm!"

"We've got to go," decided Freddie, jumping to the ground. He seemed to have completely forgotten about the suspicious rustling noises. The vision of the medal for bravery had banished all other thoughts. Eddie had no choice but to follow his brother. He slid down the rough bark and cautiously placed his feet on the ground, listening attentively.

The forest was silent. But it was an illusory silence. That's how it always seems when a lull follows a dreadful din. The storm had passed. Now it was just purring somewhere in the distance. The trees were shaking off the raindrops that had pooled on their green crowns, letting them fall quietly onto the damp earth. The wind had dropped and the night suddenly seemed blacker than before.

"I want to go home," said Eddie in a whisper, and immediately felt very ashamed.

But what a surprise—Freddie didn't leap at the chance to mock his brother! What's more, he had no intention of doing so. He took him by the hand, and in a soft, very un-Freddie-like tone he said, "Come on!" and tugged him forwards. "Come on!" he said again. "We've got to find Clementine."

They walked in single file, instinctively dodging the dangling wet branches. As they reached an unfamiliar glade, it suddenly became light. The moon had broken through the ragged layer of clouds and turned the wet forest silver. The boys stood still, holding hands.

"Like in a fairy tale, isn't it?" murmured Freddie, and gave a loud sneeze because something had tickled his nose.

"Look!" whispered Eddie, squeezing his brother's hand.

"Where?"

"There! There! Can't you see it?" Eddie tugged his brother's sleeve.

"I can't see anything!" snapped Freddie.

"There's a light!"

"Aha!" Now Freddie could also see a faint, distant glow hidden in the thicket.

"A house? Out here?" Eddie was so surprised he almost sat on the ground.

"Come on, let's go and see who lives in it. Maybe Clementine has found shelter there."

They set off. To reach the source of the mysterious light they had to leave the path. They forced their way through dense bushes until finally they were standing in front of a wooden house, barely visible among the thick spruce trees. The moon had hidden behind the clouds again, and it was very dark.

"Wait here," whispered Freddie. "I'll try to peep through the window."

"No, I'm not staying on my own!" Eddie raised his voice almost to a shout.

"Ssshh! Don't yell like that!"

Freddie tiptoed over to the wooden wall of the house. He tried to peek through the window, but there was no chance. It was too high up. The bright rectangle of the window gave out a yellowish glow amid the dark wall of wooden logs.

"Can you see anything?" whispered Eddie from his hiding place.

"Nothing. The window's too high."

"Wait, I'll give you a leg-up," offered Eddie.

"OK! Just be careful. Don't make so much noise," warned Freddie, clambering onto his brother's curved back.

"Wait, there's a big beam here, I'll stand on it."

Eddie was puffing and panting under the weight of Freddie's body, and that was probably the only reason why he didn't hear the sound of footsteps creeping up on them from around the corner.

"Can you see anything?" he asked, having a hard time catching his breath.

"There's a strange room," muttered Freddie, leaning on one knee, "with lots of antlers on the walls..."

"Got you, you rascals!" a deep voice suddenly bellowed right above their heads, while at the same time two strong hands grabbed hold of them. Freddie slid off Eddie's back onto the ground and hardly knew what was going on as their unknown assailant pushed him and his petrified brother into a strange, cramped little space.

"What's going on? Who are you?" cried Freddie, struggling.

"Where are you putting us?" roared Eddie.

"Where? You dare to ask? In the shed! You'll sit there until morning and then I'll take you to the police station!"

"Why the police station?" cried Eddie, wriggling in the man's tight grip.

"You have no right to imprison us," shouted Freddie angrily.

"All right, all right! We'll find out tomorrow who has the right to do what!" That was the last they heard before the crash of a bolt being shut.

"What the devil!" whispered Freddie. "Who was that?"

"How should I know?" whimpered Eddie.

"Don't howl! That won't help us in the least," said Freddie, making a futile attempt to grapple with the bolt. "Looks like we can't get out of here!"

"But what was he on about, that man?" muttered Eddie, trying to find a more comfortable spot in the cramped shed. "Who did he think we were?"

"Exactly. Who on earth?"

7.

In which Sergeant Beeper grows
increasingly worried, and Constable
Podger lands in a ditch

===

THE SERGEANT WALKED HOME BRISKLY. HE WAS
thinking about the events that had dragged him from
his warm bed on this strangely unsettled night. He
urgently needed to know the details. Maybe he should
try phoning the police station in town again? Maybe
they'd realized that the line had been damaged and
had managed to fix it by now. Hmm... actually, it would
probably take a few days before they were reconnected
with the big police station. Just two weeks ago it had
taken five whole days to find a damaged cable in the
forest. Such was the fate of the village police station
in St Jude's!

Sergeant Beeper rubbed his cheek, which since his morning shave had already covered itself in short, spiky stubble. He looked up at the sky and frowned—as long as the heavens didn't open before Podger reached town! He pushed open the garden gate and stopped by the kennel. There was nothing moving inside. "Asleep? Huh, a fine guard dog he is!" he said to himself, and smiled at the mere thought of Pickles's funny snout. He tiptoed to his room to avoid waking Teddy. The moment he switched on a small lamp, a sudden gust of wind blew the wooden shutter open with a crash.

"Hell!" grunted the sergeant, battling the increasing gale, which was flinging piles of paper around the room.

"Drat and double drat!" The shutter refused to close, and the sergeant had a lengthy struggle before he was able to fasten the hooks in the right places. At that very moment the telephone on his desk began making a weird noise, like a croaking frog:

RRRRIBBIT! RRRRIBBIT!

The sergeant reached the desk in a single bound.

"Hellooo!"

Silence. Only from far, far away, as if from beyond seven hills and forests, came the sound of the rising wind. And then that noise again.

"Hello! This is Beeper! Helloo!"

"Sergeant, there's a problem with the line, you need to..." The voice from the receiver broke off completely, and all he could hear was a strange hum.

The sergeant ran a hand through his ruffled hair. A network of deep wrinkles covered his brow. "There's new information," he thought feverishly. "They must want to tell me something important, but I can't hear a thing!" He tapped on the telephone cradle a few times.

"The child went... Clementine..." He heard the distant voice of the constable again.

"I know! Into the forest! But where exactly? The forest covers almost twenty square kilometres!" cried Beeper, wiping his sweaty brow. "And who is this Clementine?"

"It's..." There was silence again, broken by a faint burble.

"Who? Spell it out, I can't hear a thing!"

"Listen! Write down..." came the indistinct words. "Clementine is..."

This time a rumble of thunder went rolling across the sky, and once it was quiet again the telephone was as silent as the grave. The sergeant tapped the cradle a few more times, but to no avail. The receiver dangled from his desk, swinging on its cable, as the sergeant gnashed his teeth and poured out all his rage onto a piece of headed notepaper. Just then Constable Podger ran in, buttoning up his uniform, and shouted from the doorway: "Give me the report! I'm off!"

"Shhhh..." hissed Sergeant Beeper. "You'll wake Teddy! I've just spoken with the police station again," he added in a milder tone, "but I couldn't understand a thing. Well, go on, get a move on!" he suddenly shouted, but with a glance at Teddy's bedroom, he lowered his voice. "A child is wandering about somewhere in the forest! On her own, at night!"

Constable Podger grabbed the report from the sergeant's hands and ran to the door.

"Take my coat," added the sergeant. "It's going to pour."

Podger nodded, and moments later the sergeant heard the whirr of the battered old motorbike. Then everything fell silent.

The wind was yanking at the shutter again, trying to rip out the hook along with part of the frame. A rumble of thunder rolled across the navy-blue sky. The sergeant looked anxiously through the window. The gale was gathering force. The pine trees were bending in the wind in a wild dance. The sergeant glanced at the telephone and frowned. He picked up the dangling receiver, held it to his ear for a moment, and then angrily slammed it down on the cradle.

The shutters rattled again. The sergeant tapped his fingers nervously on the desk.

Where was that poor child now? That little girl, all alone in the huge forest.

*　*　*　*

Meanwhile, Constable Podger had just turned off the narrow country lane onto the highway that led straight to town. He had thirty kilometres ahead of him, but that was nothing for a brave policeman and his motorbike, which, despite occasionally "packing up", as they say, was still a faithful companion that for the most part performed well in difficult off-road conditions.

"A storm doesn't bother me!" he muttered, twisting the accelerator.

The motorbike worked away steadily, only bouncing a little on the bumpy road.

The constable was thinking about the task he had to fulfil.

On either side of him the dense forest was raging and roaring. Suddenly the heavens opened. It was so abrupt that the constable wobbled on his seat.

"Blast and damnation!" he swore, braking at the side of the road. He took out his large motorcycle goggles and put them on, to protect his face from the biting rain. He turned up the collar of the waterproof coat, silently thanking the sergeant for having thought of it. "Sergeant Beeper is a good chap," he thought to himself as he settled comfortably on the seat. "He's got a clever son, and he asked for a pay rise for me too. We work well together at our station. But what about this lost child? We need to find her at all costs!"

"Come on then, hit the road, Mr Podger!" he said out loud before kicking the clutch. The motorbike leapt into life and set off down the road, inundated by wave after wave of rain.

He was just approaching a bend on the fifth kilometre when suddenly...

CRRRAASH!!!

In a flash of lightning and a roar of thunder he saw the trunk of a wind-toppled pine tree lying right across the road. Failing to apply the brakes in time, he went into a skid and smashed straight into it. Catapulted out of his seat, the wretched Podger traced an arc through the air and landed in a roadside ditch full of mud.

"Hell and a false leg!" he muttered, clambering out of the ditch. He moved his arms and legs. All in order. No harm done. But why was it so dark? "I can't see anything!" He touched his face anxiously and breathed a sigh of relief. It was nothing—it was just that his goggles were covered in mud. He tore them off and walked over to the motorbike, which was lying close by. The engine was still running, but the front wheel was completely bent and the dashboard showed no signs of life. "That's the end of that journey," he thought to himself. In another flash of lightning he took a closer look at the fallen tree. Well, that could have ended very badly! But what should he do? Keep going on foot? Out of the question. That was a waste of time. Go back to the station? The sergeant would be angry. So what then? First and foremost, he had to complete his task. So he would go back to St Jude's and take the jeep. Yes, but first that tree had to be removed somehow. Somebody might come driving along here, and this was a disaster waiting to happen.

It was raining cats and dogs. The constable dragged the wrecked motorbike to the edge of the road.

"What a shame about the motorbike! I'll take it to be repaired but it'll be months before they fix it. This storm is the devil's work!" he muttered, walking around the fallen trunk.

He grabbed one of the branches and tried to shift the tree. Heavy. He dug in his heels and pulled. It moved. The constable stopped and wiped the sweat from his brow. As the gale raged around him, he yanked at the heavy trunk again. This time he was more successful. Fortunately, this pine tree wasn't one of the biggest.

"An axe would be helpful. Then I could cut off the branches. But there's nothing for it. I'll have to drag it at least as far as the verge."

He grabbed a branch again and dragged it across the road with such force that his eyes filled with tears. He stopped, panting loudly and wiping his brow, before setting to work again. Just a bit more effort and the obstacle blocking the road would be out of the way. The constable sat down on the trunk, wheezing heavily. Some adventure he was having! The dense clouds melted away for a moment, revealing a huge silver moon.

The constable glanced at the mangled motorbike lying nearby. Oh well, he'd have to go back on foot! But not by the highway, because it was the long way. He knew a path through the forest that was a shortcut to the village. But what should he do with the bike? "Never mind, I'll leave it here until tomorrow." He stood up, broke off some pine branches, and used them to camouflage the vehicle.

The clouds had covered the sky again, and it was pitch black. The constable looked about him and set off. In a few paces he had jumped across the roadside ditch and entered the forest. He hadn't gone far when suddenly he heard a noise coming from the road. What was that? Was someone coming this way? Moments later, he could clearly hear the sound of an engine. A car? Out here, in the backwoods, late at night? Maybe it was going to town? Instantly the constable turned on his heel and ran towards the road. The engine noise was coming closer, growing louder. Stumbling, the constable ran as fast as the heavy raincoat would let him. Now he could see a streak of light from the approaching vehicle in the distance. "I won't make it," he thought desperately. He dashed up to the road just in time to see a red car passing the fallen trunk.

"Hey! Hello!!!" he yelled, but his voice was lost in the roar of the engine. "Wait!" he bellowed again and threw himself after the car.

But the driver couldn't hear him. The constable stamped his foot in silent rage.

That was bad luck. Such dreadful, awful bad luck could only happen to him, Podger. If only he had stayed by the road, if only he hadn't started walking back through the forest! But how could he have guessed that a vehicle would appear on this rarely frequented road? And in the middle of a tempest! "Who the devil was that?" he wondered about the driver of the red car. "No one round here has a car like that—it must be one of the holidaymakers." He shook his head, and only then realized that he was still wearing the heavy motorbike helmet.

"Too bad!" he said, undoing the chin strap. "I'll just have to walk."

And he plunged into the forest again.

8.

In which Mr Ignatius Prosser
sleeps through a worthy
subject for an article

===

THE RED CAR WENT RACING ALONG THE FOREST
road, splashing through the puddles. The two narrow
beams of the headlights lit up the dense blackness of the
night. It was still raining non-stop, as though someone
way up high were pouring down bucket after bucket of
water. Behind the wheel, Mr Prosser was staring intently
into the opaque darkness. Streams of rain were running
down his face, soaking into his coat and dribbling in
cold trickles down his spine. Despite the protective
goggles he was wearing, the water was seeping into his
eyes, making it harder to drive the car. It was easy to
define the visibility: there wasn't any.

"I should slow down," he thought, and reduced his speed, although the car began grunting again. "If only I had a roof!" The vision of the forester's lodge and the supper that awaited him there faded, and was swept away by the streams of water coming at him sideways.

In fact, Mr Prosser couldn't have cared less which roof provided him with shelter. Any kind of protection from the downpour would do.

"It's a good thing the car's still going!" he muttered, and instantly realized that there was no wood for him to knock on.

Mr Prosser was actually one of those people who are terribly superstitious, and he knocked on wood whenever circumstances required. This time, not only was there no unpainted wood within reach, but more importantly, he couldn't take his hands off the steering wheel for a single moment.

His fears were groundless. Though the forest track was not a road of the best quality, the little red car was freely racing along it, and it was only his state of extreme dampness that was prompting some despondency in its driver.

The thunder was booming, and time and again flashes of lightning cut through the menacing blackness of the sky.

Suddenly, an uprooted tree at the side of the road briefly appeared in the light of his headlamps. Mr Prosser whistled in surprise and slowed down even more. "How lucky that tree didn't fall across the road!" he said to himself, and broke out in a cold sweat at the mere thought of what would have happened to him and his car if that had been the case. "What terrible dangers lie in wait for drivers during a storm! I'll go to the town," he decided. "I'll never be able to find the forester's lodge tonight."

He drove another dozen kilometres through thick forest. Then the trees thinned, and the car came out

... AND BROKE OUT IN A COLD SWEAT

on a winding road through some meadows that smelt strongly of damp grass. The moon emerged briefly from behind the clouds, revealing a sight for Mr Prosser's sore eyes: the distant, still hazy rooftops of the houses in the town. So he sped up, and shortly after arrived among the first buildings.

"I wonder if I can find a room in a hotel here?" he thought as he turned down a narrow street.

The town was dark and silent. The low, slightly sunken cottages stood in a tight row, with their wooden shutters closed to the world.

"How can people sleep through such a storm?" mused Mr Prosser, searching for a suitable place to park his car. Looking carefully to left and right, he suddenly noticed a house with a sign, large but still illegible at this distance, above the entrance.

"That must be a hotel!" he rejoiced, and pulled up to the kerb. He switched off the motor and removed his goggles. But when he got out of the car, happily stretching his legs as he took a step closer, he realized that his hopes had been premature! In black letters on the white sign it said:

POLICE STATION

"Oh blast!" muttered Mr Prosser, taking off his soaking-wet coat. "I've never spent the night at a police station before!"

He knocked on the door. Silence. He tried the handle. The door opened with a loud creak. Mr Prosser went inside and immediately tripped over some kind of metal object, which clanged loudly.

"Who's there?" boomed a voice, and the burly figure of an oak-tree-sized policeman appeared in the illumin-ated doorway.

"Good evening," said Mr Prosser politely as he stepped into the room. "I'm a journalist, the storm caught me out on the road, and now I'm looking for—"

"A hotel, probably?" said the police officer, laughing.

"Exactly," replied Mr Prosser, and he was on the point of continuing his tale about the forester's lodge when suddenly from the other room there came the bang of a falling chair and a muffled but audible curse.

Mr Prosser stopped with his mouth agape—before he'd had time to splutter a single word, the neighbouring door crashed open and there stood a second policeman, who gasped in a tone of distinct irritation: "I was cut off again! These telephones are enough to drive you mad!"

"So what's up? Didn't Beeper get the message?" asked the man-mountain with evident concern in his voice.

"I doubt he understood anything at all! I told him about the child, and the, er... Clementine, but in this situation we'll just have to carry out the operation ourselves."

"We don't have enough men," said the man-mountain, clutching his temples.

"But we can't leave a child in the forest. I've already sent Johnson to fetch some people to help. I gave him the van... He should be back any minute now!"

"Excuse me," interrupted Mr Prosser. "Has a child gone missing?"

"Yes. Oh, sir, you won't believe what we've been going through! The child's father and all the rest of them are breathing down our necks. But organizing a search is no easy task, especially as they only reported it a short time ago. And now, to make matters worse, this awful tempest has erupted! But excuse me, who are you, sir?"

"I am a journalist, Ignatius Prosser, at your service! I lost my way in the storm. I was supposed to be spending the night somewhere else entirely, but my car broke down on the road... Now I'm looking for a hotel around here!"

"Very nice to meet you, sir! I am Sergeant Whiskers. This is Constable Muggins. Unfortunately, there's no hotel in our town," said the sergeant, spreading his hands in a silent gesture of despair.

"That's bad luck!" muttered Mr Prosser and slumped down on a wooden chair.

"Perhaps you'd like a cup of tea, sir?" asked Muggins, noticing their guest's sodden clothes. "A hot cup of tea will do you good!"

"Thank you. Thank you very much," mumbled Mr Prosser, looking almost affectionately at the giant. "So what's become of this child?"

"Well, quite! That's exactly what we'd like to know! The child went missing in the forest about thirty kilometres from here. Near the village of St Jude's. They made a stop there…" The sergeant suddenly broke off, interrupted by the clear sound of a phone ringing in the other room.

"Goodness me!" cried Muggins, placing a cup of hot tea in front of the journalist. "Goodness me! That must be the station in St Jude's calling!"

Sergeant Whiskers was at the phone in one leap.

"Hellloo! Yes. No, not yet. We're organizing people… Of course! Yes, we'll let you know immediately, sir," said the sergeant, anxiously tapping his cigarette case against the tabletop.

"That was the girl's father," he muttered, drawing deeply on his cigarette.

Mr Prosser leant against the table and closed his eyes. Utter exhaustion was seeping out of his every pore. All the trouble with the car, and the toing and froing in the middle of the storm—that was quite enough! He was completely spent. Not even the steaming cup of tea could boost his strength—quite the opposite, it was intensifying the drowsiness that was coming over him.

"I just have to last until morning," he muttered, swaying on his chair. "A child? A missing child..." said his sluggish mind. "Wait a minute, that's incredibly important!" Mr Prosser woke up so abruptly that he very nearly overturned the empty cup. He must go with the police officers! He could take a few people in his car. Then he'd write a brilliant article about it!

"Would you please tell me, gentlemen," he cried, leaping to his feet, "how it actually happened?"

"Well, it's basically a very ordinary story—"

"Sergeant! St Jude's on the line!" Muggins suddenly shouted, tapping on the cradle.

"Well done, Constable! I'm just coming!" called the sergeant, running out of the room.

Mr Prosser fell back onto the chair. From behind the closed door he could hear voices having a conversation. He tried to eavesdrop out of curiosity, but couldn't understand a word of it. The sergeant was shouting something, losing his temper. Suddenly the conversation stopped, and all Mr Prosser could hear was nervous tapping on the telephone cradle. He stood up from the uncomfortable chair and looked around the room. Under the window there was an old armchair upholstered with faded red cloth. With a sigh of relief, he sat down in the armchair and leant his head against the soft backrest. At last he felt warm and very comfortable.

Moments later, when the constable came back into the room, he noticed that the unknown night-time visitor was sound asleep.

"What should we do with him, Sergeant?"

"What should we do? Well, we can't throw a man out onto the street in the middle of the night! We'll shut that room, and we'll tell Johnson to stay here and keep an eye on him."

"Yes, sir!" said the constable, clicking his heels in military style.

"This traveller has his rights too. He has to rest somewhere!"

"Particularly when we can't suggest a more suitable place for him. Come on, Muggins, let's go! I'll drop in on them again..."

"Them? Meaning those people with the tents?"

"Of course! I think we're going to have to take that whole crazy company with us..." He glanced at the sleeping man and lowered his voice.

They left the room, closing the door quietly behind them.

*　*　*　*

Dawn was peeking in through the windows when Mr Ignatius Prosser awoke from a deep sleep. He opened his eyes, blinked, opened them again and carefully looked around him. "Where on earth am I?" he wondered. "Whose room is this?" He stood up from the armchair, stretched and yawned deeply. It took him a while to remember his experiences of the previous night. So he had been calmly sleeping here while the police were looking for a missing child! That was terrible! Scandalous! What kind of a reporter just falls asleep at the crucial moment, like a... like a dormouse?! "Out there in the darkness they were carrying out a forest-combing operation, as that friendly giant put it, and here I was, snoring!" Mr Prosser reproached himself. He went over to the window and gave a long whistle. Day was already breaking! A vision of Mr Twisk, his dear friend who was waiting for him with breakfast, suddenly flashed through his mind, so vividly that it made Mr Prosser blink. His tummy was rumbling with hunger, drumming out an impressive early-morning march. Breakfast! Once in his head, that was a thought he couldn't escape. Though perhaps he ought to join the search party? But which direction should he take? The police officers hadn't said anything...

Mr Prosser looked distastefully at his clothes, which were still wet, and his crumpled coat, then anxiously scratched at his stubbly chin. Well, too bad—he had to go. He had to reach the eagerly anticipated forester's lodge at last! He stepped away from the window and took his

HIS
STUBBLY
CHIN

coat off the rack. He quietly opened the door into the hallway and looked about to see which way to go. Where was the exit? He took a step forward and tripped on a metal object lying on the floor.

"Who's there?" A young lad in a police uniform leant out of the neighbouring room.

"Drat! Another police officer! What if he refuses to let me go?" Mr Prosser thought in horror, and stopped.

"Ah, it's you, sir! Did you sleep well?" asked the lad cheerfully.

"Yes. Thank you for your hospitality," mumbled Mr Prosser. "Do you know where the sergeant and the other policeman went?"

"They've been out on the operation for a long time," smiled the lad. "I advise you to go and have some breakfast, sir. Although... where could you go at this time of the morning? The pub's still closed... I'm afraid I have nothing to offer you, sir!"

"Never mind," sighed Mr Prosser. "I'll manage. Goodbye... Thank you for letting me stay the night."

"You're welcome! A night in a police station isn't usually a fond memory!"

Mr Prosser went over to his mud-spattered car, which was patiently waiting by the side of the road.

"Oh dear!" he moaned. "It needs a bit of a wash!" Fortunately, right in the middle of the sleepy market square there was a pump. With the help of a wet rag, the "red calamity" was soon looking more or less acceptable again. "But will it start? Will it be willing to do as it's told?" mused the journalist, slumping onto the damp car seat. He switched on the engine.

"Achoo!! Achoo!" sneezed the car, and after a few minutes that to Mr Prosser seemed to last almost an eternity, it roared into life with all the power of its mechanical horses.

"Hoooraay!!!" cried Mr Prosser, waking a flock of white chickens that were sitting near the well. "We're off! But where to?" he wondered, smartly taking a left turn. "The police officers, Mr Phosphorus, the forester's lodge... Ha! We're heading into the woods!"

9.

In which Teddy finds someone, but it
soon turns out not to be Clementine

===

"OFF WE GO!" CRIED TEDDY TO PICKLES, AND THEY
raced ahead. Incredibly pleased with the unscheduled
walk, the dog kept rootling in the bushes and then
leaping back onto the path, barking.

"Shh, boy! Quiet!" Teddy warned him, but much less
firmly, because by now they were very far from the risky
houses. And just then the terrible storm broke out.

Pickles was whimpering a little from fear, keeping
close to Teddy's legs.

"Don't be afraid, boy! Nothing awful's going to
happen!" Teddy comforted him, as he too struggled
against the violent gusts of wind.

It was getting nasty. Time and again, the darkness

was interrupted by sharp flashes of lightning and booming thunder, none of which was much help for Teddy's detective work. As he shielded his face against the sharp twigs and pine cones that were being swept about by the wind, he was dreaming of Sherlock Holmes's cosy study, because he had always imagined that any extraordinary investigative operation should really be solved in a deep, comfortable armchair. "A club armchair, ideally," he thought, sheltering the shivering dog with his entire body. Well, yes. But he was the one who had come up with "Operation Clementine" just a couple of hours ago, and then decided to look for the girl in the forest at night.

But he wasn't afraid of the storm. He had grown up in the countryside and was used to being in permanent contact with nature, and so he treated all forms of weather as a necessary good or evil, inextricably linked to their proper time of year. In winter he would wade cheerfully through the snowdrifts, and in spring he would sink into sticky mud, struggling to pull his slightly oversized wellington boots out of the mire. And now a storm! But an extremely sudden and thundery one. There went another bolt of lightning! Poor Pickles, who turned out not to be quite so indifferent to the storm, was making himself smaller and smaller, curling into a ball and squeezing his nose between his paws, as if he wasn't a large, self-respecting German shepherd, but a miniature pinscher on legs like matchsticks. As he fought with the branches that kept whacking him hard on the nose, Teddy did his best to soothe the terrified beast by talking to him in a calm tone.

CRASSHHH!

Wow, that one had struck close by! For a split second Teddy saw a burning, blue streak that cut across the sky. At the same time a loud crash rang out, and the whole forest began to shudder. Pickles's whimpering grew louder as he turned circles, chasing his own tail. A trickle of cold sweat went down Teddy's spine. It was a truly terrifying sight. Now they were both afraid, the boy and his dog. Teddy knew that during a storm you mustn't stand under a tree, because lightning usually strikes trees. He knew it. But the fear that had suddenly crept into the young detective's heart, so brave until now, paralysed him, making any kind of action impossible. Everything around him was thundering and booming. The whole forest was shaking to its foundations, and it felt as if any moment now the swaying pine trees would topple like ninepins, burying the terrified boy and his dog among their branches.

Teddy couldn't really tell how long the storm lasted. When he finally crawled out of the undergrowth, soaked to the skin, the rain had stopped and the storm was moving into the distance, only turning the dark forest green from time to time. And just then, Teddy noticed that Pickles was missing!

He set off at a run, feverishly scouring the wet bushes. But it was no good. He'd vanished into thin air! "What should I do?" wondered Teddy, wiping the water off his eyelashes. "Go on alone? Pickles is sure to turn up, but what if he's been squashed by a falling tree?" He had heard a suspicious crash in the distance. The poor doggie! For a while Teddy considered what to do next. Go back home? For shame! He'd left Dad such a great report! He'd thought up the operation—he was the most brilliant detective in the entire region, and who knows, perhaps even in the whole country! And he was going to give up? Never! Teddy would save his honour as a detective and the honour of the whole police force! So onwards he would go!

He looked around him. It was dark and wet. Above him ripples of wind were shaking raindrops off the trees. Teddy switched on his torch. In the beam of light he saw some green ferns straightening their feathery fronds, which the rain had pressed to the ground. There were bushes and tree trunks, but no sign of the dog. He whistled softly. Then louder. No answer. Silence. With a sigh, he brushed aside a lock of hair that was stuck to his forehead. He looked about him once again, and then another time, and headed off decisively.

All of a sudden, for no apparent reason, he sensed that there was someone else in the forest apart from him. He really couldn't have explained where exactly this certainty came from. He stopped on the path and switched the torch on again. There was nobody there! But he thought he could hear voices amid the faint soughing of the wind. He whistled again. The bushes to his left shook violently and a large shadow leapt onto the path. Before Teddy had a chance to be truly scared, the black shadow jumped into his arms, whining with joy.

"Pickles! You old rascal!" cried Teddy with delight, abruptly leaning away from the big warm tongue that was desperately trying to lick his nose. "OK, OK, that's enough! The main thing is that you've turned up," he muttered, struggling to regain his balance. "Now, boy, let's go and look for Clementine together!"

The dog set off behind Teddy obediently, though with strange reluctance. For some time they walked in complete silence. With his nose to the ground, the dog was following a scent. From time to time he would disappear among the trees, but then come straight back to the path. Suddenly he stopped, stretched his neck and gave a short growl.

"What's up?" asked Teddy curiously, shining his torch. He looked around him, but couldn't see anything.

He wanted to keep going, but this time the dog wouldn't budge, and was growling softly. The thick clouds crowding the sky melted away for a moment, and the boy suddenly caught a glimpse of a strange, almost unreal light, just a few steps from the path.

"What's that?" he wondered, and looked again. "Yes, it's a tree trunk, but there's something shining inside it!"

It wasn't fire, because the light was dim and purplish-green in colour. He took a couple more steps forwards. How strange! He pointed the torch upwards. The glow faded and went out. In the black trunk he could see a large hollow, and in it...

"It's her!" spluttered Teddy, shaken by the unexpected discovery. "It's Clementine!" he whispered, and grabbing Pickles by the muzzle he went up to the mysterious tree.

Inside the hollow, on a layer of soft woodchips, which was the source of that mysterious glow in the darkness, sat... a little girl. The torchlight must have given her a fright, because she had jumped up abruptly, hitting her head painfully.

"What's that? Who are you?" she stammered fearfully, looking at the strange boy who was shining a torch right into her eyes.

"Switch that off this second!" she demanded, rubbing the top of her aching head.

"Clementine!" cried Teddy with delight.

"Where? Where's Clementine?" asked the girl, suddenly coming to her senses.

"What do you mean: where?" asked Teddy in surprise. "You're Clementine, the girl I'm looking for!"

"Me?" said the girl, opening her eyes wide. "I'm called Annie!"

"What do you mean, Annie?"

"Just what I say. My name is Annie. And I'm looking for Clementine!"

"Wait a moment," said Teddy. "I was the one who overheard Dad's conversation about the missing girl! That was secret information!"

"Some secret!" snorted Annie, cautiously climbing out of the hollow. "We've known about it for ages!"

"We?" asked Teddy in surprise. "You're not alone?"

"I am now. But I wasn't earlier on."

"I don't understand at all," said Teddy, watching with curiosity as Annie slid down from the tree. "Do you know where Clementine is?"

"No, I don't," she called back, jumping nimbly to the ground. "Maybe Mark has found her... or Pudding."

"What pudding? What are you talking about?"

"Not what but who! Pudding is a boy—and what's more he's my brother! So is Mark."

"Ah. But where are they?"

"I don't know. They got lost during the storm. I was walking along with them, and then suddenly there was a bolt of lightning, everything turned green, and that's when they vanished from sight! Is that your dog?"

"Yes!" Teddy puffed out his chest proudly. "His name is Pickles!"

"Pleased to meet you," said Annie automatically. Mum always paid great attention to so-called good manners.

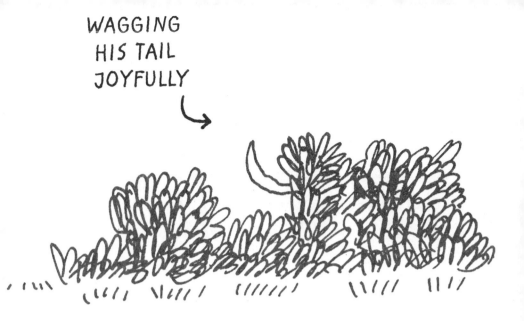

WAGGING
HIS TAIL
JOYFULLY

"He's pleased too," replied Teddy gallantly, and finally let Pickles go.

"So what shall we do?" asked Annie, stroking the dog's wet head. "It's night-time and it's so hard to see..."

"That doesn't matter. We must carry on with the search. I mean... *I* must!"

"What about me? Am I supposed to stay here?" said Annie indignantly. "I'm coming too! After all, my brothers are somewhere around here..."

They disentangled themselves from the undergrowth and went back to the familiar path. Pickles ran on ahead, wagging his tail joyfully. After a while he stopped, pricked up his ears and raced off.

"He's scented something," said Teddy, coming to a stop.

"Let's creep over in that direction," suggested Annie, and set off without making a sound.

Not a single twig crackled beneath her feet. "Like a Red Indian," thought Teddy, and followed in her tracks.

In silence, with the greatest caution, they reached a huge pit, at the edge of which stood Pickles. The dog was sniffing the air noisily. Then he turned in a circle and started snuffling, pushing the wet leaves about with his nose.

"Maybe there's someone there."

"Hey! Is anybody there?" called Teddy.

Silence. Only the trees rustled.

"There's no one there," said Teddy, squatting down. "But I bet there was someone."

"Do you think they've gone already?"

"Look what that dog's up to."

Pickles had his nose to the ground and was running towards the path.

"Maybe it's a bear's den?" said Annie, lowering her voice to a whisper.

"What? It's such a massive pit!"

They walked in silence for some time, Teddy in front with his torch and the dog, and Annie following behind him.

"You know what," said Annie, "I wish it was already light. And I wish Mark and Pudding would turn up."

"And I wish I'd found Clementine by now, taken her back to Dad at the police station and been able to say, 'Officer Beeper Junior, reporting a find!'"

"I don't think a person can be a find," mused Annie.

"What can they be then?"

"Er, maybe... reporting an achievement?"

"Hmm, but Clementine isn't an achievement either! Anyway, it doesn't matter what I say. The look on Dad's face will be the most important thing!"

"Oh dear!" moaned Annie. "And what will my dad's face look like when he finds out about our nocturnal expedition?"

"Are you afraid?"

"No, Dad only gets back tomorrow—but what if Mark and Pudding don't turn up?"

"They're sure to turn up," said Teddy, comforting her.

"This forest is big, but it's not so massive that you could get lost in it for ever."

"I think we're lost too," mumbled Annie, tripping over a protruding tree root.

"But we're not! There's a hut not far from here. Do you want to go there?"

"Yes!"

"OK," agreed Teddy, who was feeling very tired by now. "Just look out for roots. Actually, you'd better give me your hand, we have to leave the path here."

Annie was very tired and sleepy too. Hanging on to Teddy tightly, she battled through the tangle of roots and bushes, dreaming of a nice soft bed. Her damp dress was sticking to her body, restricting her movements. Pickles ran alongside them, panting loudly.

They reached the hut on their last legs. Teddy squeezed in first through the low entrance. He shone his torch. It was empty. In the corner lay a bundle of hay, and on a wooden bench stood a candle stuck into the neck of a bottle. There was a box of matches lying next to it, and a pot on the shelf. Teddy looked inside it hopefully.

"Empty!" he said regretfully. "There's nothing to eat."

"But there is somewhere to sleep," said Annie, sighing with relief as she buried herself in the fragrant hay.

Teddy followed suit. Pickles flopped down with a bump next to Teddy and laid his head on his knees. A moment later, the hut was completely silent.

10.

In which, despite the late hour, Mark
and Pudding scrape the frying pan clean

===

"THOSE ARE DEFINITELY A WOLF'S EYES," SAID
Pudding and squeezed his eyelids tightly shut. He sat
still for a while, his heart beating hard. "Is... is it still
there?" he whispered, opening one eye.

Mark didn't reply. As if hypnotized, he was staring
at the green spots that were shining above the edge of
the pit.

"Answer me," said Pudding, who was blubbering for
real. "Is it still watching us?"

"No, it's stopped," said Mark with a lump in his
throat. And he decided he should do something immediately to stop being scared. And to calm Pudding down
too. His baby brother was wet, terrified and probably

freezing. He looked like a little mouse. Mark moved his numb leg.

"What's up? What's up?" stammered Pudding, clutching at Mark's elbow.

"Nothing. It's gone!" replied Mark in a cheerful tone.

"Take another look," insisted Pudding.

"I'm telling you, there's nothing there."

Mark slowly crawled out from underneath their shelter. It had stopped raining now, but in the meantime a large, very sticky puddle had formed at the bottom of the pit, in which last year's pine cones were drowning. Mark rubbed his stiff thighs and craned his neck in an effort to see what was happening in the ever-quieter forest. It was dark, dark as pitch. Fortunately, the green eyes had gone.

"Come on out, Pudding!"

"Why? It's quite cosy in here," squeaked Pudding, retreating deeper into the pit. Though cramped, the hole still seemed to offer perfectly good protection from anything that might happen outside.

Mark peered into the distance, looking for a way out of the trap they had landed in quite by accident.

"Pudding!" he snapped. "Do you hear me? Come out immediately, if you don't want to catch pneumonia!"

"And what if I do?"

"Then suit yourself! I'll leave you here, while I go and look for Annie, Clementine or anything else to be found in this damned forest by myself!"

"Don't swear," said Pudding solemnly, crawling out from under the shelter.

"Who's swearing?" asked Mark in surprise.

"You said 'damned forest', and that's an expletion..."

"Expletive. The word is 'expletive'," said Mark, struggling to dig the toes of his sandals into the steep sides. "Give me your hand, I'll pull you up."

"But I don't want to!" screamed Pudding, falling into the puddle with a splash.

"See? Now you'll be completely wet," moaned Mark, who was standing in a very uncomfortable position. "And you won't be able to crawl over here by yourself!"

"I'll hold on to a branch," replied Pudding, fighting back tears.

"Go ahead then, just don't bawl! If you're going to howl, I'm leaving you here," Mark said angrily, though perfectly aware that it was a nasty piece of blackmail; he wouldn't abandon his little brother in the forest in any circumstances.

"I don't believe you," whimpered Pudding, because he too was well aware that Mark would never do that.

Suddenly the clouds parted and bright moonlight flooded the forest.

"It's weird here," exclaimed Pudding, and in a single leap landed beside his brother.

"Look! Now you can see our pit as clear as day! Come this way," called Mark, pulling himself upwards. "Hold on to these branches!"

Pudding was panting and the slippery soles of his shoes kept sliding down. Finally, he grabbed hold of Mark's trousers.

By the time they had made it back onto the path, the clouds had covered the sky again.

"I'm hungry," said Pudding, finally letting go of his brother.

"It's a pity we didn't bring any supplies with us," sighed Mark sadly, feeling the gnawing pain of hunger in his stomach. "We couldn't have foreseen it!"

"Foreseen what? That I'd be hungry?"

"No, you're always hungry! We couldn't have foreseen the storm, and..."

"And what?" nagged Pudding.

"And, you know, that we'd be outside for such a long time. I thought we'd find Clementine close to where we found Macadamia. That was my brilliant plan..."

"Yeah, really brilliant," muttered his brother.

"And now we can't find Annie or Clementine. And what's more, they're girls. Girls are always scared."

"Does that mean I'm not scared?" said Pudding, somewhat surprised, then at once took Mark's word for it. Pudding always believed what he wanted to believe.

Mark stood on the path, wondering which direction they should take. He had no doubt about the fact that he had to continue searching. But which way should they go? Fortunately, the moon had floated out from behind the clouds again and the whole forest was now brighter.

"Over there!" he said, pointing to a young copse.

"It's all the same to me," replied Pudding, in his shrillest voice.

"What's up?" asked Mark, who did know his little brother very well.

"Nnnothing at all," said Pudding, studiously digging a toe into the soft ground.

"Come on, spit it out!" insisted Mark.

"It's just that... well, perhaps spending so long out in the cold isn't good for us?"

"What's got into your head?" asked Mark in surprise, because Pudding had sounded just like their mum. He'd even used the same words that Mum did on similar occasions. "Are you cold?"

"No, but... but that's not the way home!" he finally spluttered.

"How do you know which way is home? You can't even remember which direction we came from!"

"But I can!" said Pudding, offended. "Because we fell into the pit straight from the path—you see? There are bushes and trees on that side, so we couldn't have fallen in from there, and we definitely have to go this way to reach the spruce trees..."

"And your bed, right?" said Mark angrily. "What about the girls? Are we just going to leave them in the forest on their own? And go home without Annie and Clementine?"

"I never said anything about my bed!" said Pudding, smearing mud and pine needles all over his face. "I was just thinking of having something to eat, and then I could come back here..."

"Come on!" said Mark and set off. "You're the most tedious child I know! I'm starting to regret ever taking you with us!"

Pudding didn't say another word. He toddled obediently in the direction of the young copse. Soon after the boys found themselves in a large clearing, shining silver in the moonlight.

"Look!" cried Pudding. "There's a house over there!"

"So there is. And there's a light on."

"Hooraay!! There'll be food!" yelped the little boy, hopping with joy.

"Let's go! Maybe Annie's in there? And maybe... Clementine?"

The boys turned to the right, and wading up to their knees through thick, wet grass, they came to some silver spruces surrounding a two-storey wooden house.

"The light is on downstairs," said Mark. "But where's the front door?"

"I think it's on the other side," replied Pudding and raced off to have a look.

"Wait! Wait!" called Mark. "We don't even know who lives here."

Pudding came to an abrupt stop. He was going so fast that he nearly went crashing into a tree.

"Surely not a witch," he stammered, and started to retreat to a safe distance.

"How childish you are!" said Mark, laughing. "You believe in dwarves and witches! Shh..." he suddenly whispered, grabbing him by the arm.

"What is it? I don't want to hear anything at all," whispered Pudding, blocking his ears.

"There are noises coming from that shed..."

"Let's go into the house! I'd rather do that now!"

Mark strode confidently up to the door. He knocked. No answer. Silence.

"Maybe there's no one at home," whined Pudding.

In response, from the depths of the house came a clatter, and then the sound of heavy footsteps.

"I'm scaaaared!" wailed the little boy, clinging to his brother's arm.

"Who's there?" boomed a voice.

"It's me, Mark! And Pudding..." said the boy, his voice trembling slightly.

The bolt rattled as it was slid aside. In the doorway stood a tall man in a paint-spattered smock.

"We lost our way... there was a storm..." said Pudding quickly at the sight of the man's frown.

"We were looking for a little girl. She's lost in the woods," explained Mark feverishly, "and then there was this terrible storm, and we fell into a pit—"

"Hold on, one thing at a time," interrupted the man, stepping back into the hallway. "Come inside. You must be soaked through!"

Mark and Pudding found themselves in a large, bizarrely furnished room. The walls and ceiling were made of thick pine logs. Under the window there was a table and a long wooden bench. Along the walls, as far as the eye could see, there were stacks of paintings leaning against each other. Some had the painted side turned to face the wall.

THE
BOLT
RATTLED

Pudding stood motionless, staring as though bewitched. Every single painting showed one and the same thing: mushrooms!

"Are you a painter, sir?" asked Mark.

"Yes. I forgot to introduce myself. My name is Twisk. Phosphorus Twisk. And these are my paintings! The fruit of this year's holiday!"

Mark was standing in front of a canvas depicting a colony of toadstools, with white spots on their red caps.

"It's beautiful!" cried Pudding in amazement.

"I'm pleased to hear it," replied the painter modestly, and suddenly froze. "Good heavens!" he burst out laughing. "What's happened to you, my boy?"

Mark turned to look at Pudding too. Standing in the middle of the room in the glow of the oil lamp, the little boy looked most peculiar.

"Pudding! You're completely covered in mud!" Mark was bent double with laughter, looking at his brother's black face and hands. To top it off, there was a green sprig of spruce sticking out of his messy hair.

"Let's get you washed," said Mr Twisk, busying himself with a bucket of water.

Soon after, with a lot of help from their host, Pudding was washing off the thick shell of mud coating almost his entire body, snorting and spitting in the process.

"Quick! Dry me quickly, please, before I go rusty!" said the little boy, for whom this operation was not in the least enjoyable.

"There, there," laughed the artist, drying off Pudding with a rough towel. "You're probably hungry too."

"And how!" cried the little boy, breaking free of the artist's hold.

"He'd do nothing but eat, but he never wants to wash his hands before sitting down at table," said Mark, rolling up his sleeves.

"Because before now I didn't know why you have to wash," muttered Pudding, inspecting the paintings.

"And now you do?" asked Mr Twisk in surprise.

"Of course! So you don't get the spoon and fork dirty!"

Mr Twisk roared with such raucous laughter that the wooden walls shook.

"You may well laugh," said Pudding, feeling hurt, "but we've lost our sister and Clementine in the forest, and—"

"You've lost them?" asked Mr Twisk, sounding shocked. "So there are some little girls out in the forest? Tell me exactly what happened! We need to find them immediately!"

The boys raced each other in their attempts to tell Mr Twisk the story of everything that had happened since they first found little Macadamia in the undergrowth.

"Well, well!" said the painter once they had finished, and placed a steaming pan in front of them. "Well, well! What plucky little boys you are! But you should have told an adult! Now you'll stay here like good children, while I go in search of this... what was her name? Ah yes, Clementine! And of course your sister, too."

"You're a good fellow, sir," said Pudding solemnly, stuffing a spoonful of food into his mouth.

The boys ate in silence. After the adventures they'd been through, the hot food and fresh brown bread tasted wonderful. When Mark had eaten his fill, he set down his spoon. Pudding was enthusiastically scraping the frying pan.

"Pudding! Behave yourself!" Mark scolded him. "Don't make such a racket!"

Pudding looked at him reproachfully.

"Perhaps you'd like some more bread?" asked Mr Twisk, gazing indulgently at the little boy as he stubbornly wrestled with the huge pan.

"No, thank you," said Pudding, "I can't eat any more. I'm already... bursting!"

"He always eats that much," sighed Mark. "But actually, sir, why weren't you asleep when we knocked?"

"I was just about to go to bed," said Mr Twisk, pulling on his wellington boots, "when I heard some thieves creeping about..."

"Thieves?" asked Pudding, his eyes open wide.

"Yes. The forester warned me that there had been some attempted break-ins here. Apparently some boys come to steal his antlers..."

"Antlers?" said Pudding in surprise.

"Of course," said Mark. "You've seen those antlers hanging on Mrs Matthews's sitting-room wall."

"So when I heard those noises and also saw someone peeping through the window, I decided to catch them. I mean, what else could they be looking for out here at night? I hid behind the corner and I caught them."

"And what did you do with them?"

"I locked them in the shed. I'll take them to the police station in the morning."

"But we came here at night too," said Mark.

"Yes, that's true. But those boys were behaving suspiciously. Anyway, I'd better go now. I'm sure the girls will turn up."

"May we stay here?" asked Pudding hopefully.

"Of course. You can sleep on my bed."

"I'm coming with you, sir," offered Mark.

"I'm not staying on my own! I won't!" roared Pudding, so loud that his voice echoed.

"You should be ashamed of yourself, Pudding! You were much braver outside in the forest."

"No," said the painter firmly. "You're both going to stay here."

"Fine. But we'll see you off."

Mr Twisk put on his coat. He stopped in the doorway and briefly listened. There was muffled banging coming from the garden shed.

"Is that the thieves?" whispered Mark.

"Hey, you in there! Be quiet!" called Mr Twisk menacingly.

"Please let us out!" they heard someone cry. "Why have you locked us up?"

"Wait," Mark whispered to Pudding. "That's... Freddie's voice!"

"Who's Freddie?" asked Mr Twisk in surprise.

Mark was already running towards the shed.

"Freddie, is that you?"

"Oh my goodness, Mark! Of course it's me! Undo the wretched bolt!"

"So they're not thieves?" Mr Twisk turned abruptly back into the hallway. In his nervous state, he couldn't remember where he'd put the keys to the shed. Finally, he found them in an empty pickled-gherkin jar.

Mark and Pudding couldn't get over their surprise.

"What are on earth you doing here?" cried Freddie.

"I should be the one asking what you're doing here! You were supposed to be sleeping in our beds and keeping an eye on Macadamia."

"So it's them," fussed Mr Twisk, struggling to fit the key in the lock.

Moments later the two prisoners were set free.

"You're right, we were supposed to be looking after her," muttered Eddie, "but we wanted to join the search for Clementine, too."

"It's not a game!" said Mark angrily. "Each of us had their own duty!"

"Quiet! Please calm down," cried Mr Twisk. "Go inside, and then you can explain everything to each other. Boys, I apologize for my mistake. If you're hungry, grab something to eat, and if you're tired"—and here Mr Twisk glanced at little Pudding—"go to bed!"

"I don't want to go to bed!" shouted Pudding. "I'd rather eat a third dinner!"

"Saint Petronilla!" sighed the painter. "Do you like fried wild mushrooms?"

"Of course!" they all cried in unison.

"Then you'll have to wait until I get home. You're tired. Quick march to bed! Lie down wherever you like. There are blankets in the cupboard. And no one is to go into the forest. Is that clear?"

"Yes!" they cried.

11.

In which Sergeant Beeper finds a clue

==

"IT'S A PITY YOU HAD TO COME BACK, PODGER," SAID the sergeant. "But at least you weren't hurt!"

"That's right! No harm done, except that I had to slave away like a lumberjack to shift that fallen tree!"

"You did very well to remove that obstacle, but who on earth was driving around here at night anyway? Maybe they've already begun the search? No, that's impossible. The car was heading for the town."

The sergeant's face clouded over. All at once his forehead was covered in a thick mesh of wrinkles. Whenever this happened, Teddy would say that his dad had a forehead like... a washboard! The sergeant sighed. At least Teddy was asleep and couldn't hear this half-whispered conversation. He stood up from the desk and walked over to the window. He pushed the shutter open. A sharp gust of air flew into the room full of blue tobacco smoke. There was no trace left of the recent storm, only the occasional patter of the last few raindrops falling from the trees.

The sergeant leant out of the window and took in a deep breath of fresh, soothing air.

The dark trunks of the pine trees stood out against the pearl-grey sky. It was just as if nothing had happened—as if there were no secrets hidden in the stormy, black night.

"Listen, Podger, I have a plan. You won't go to town. It's too late for that. We need to enlist the villagers. We'll search the forest, starting from the highway in the direction of Black Oaks until we reach that coppice near the forester's lodge."

"All right, then. The forest isn't all that dense, but a small child could get lost in it like a needle in a haystack. What if we took your dog, Sergeant?"

"Pickles? Noo," said Sergeant Beeper, laughing. "That's not a dog! It's a sheep!"

"What do you mean, a sheep?"

"Well, not literally, but that dog can't even follow the scent of a cat. He's a good old boy, but he's rather dumb. Teddy hasn't been able to train him at all. But, but... ah, it's a good thing I remembered," said the sergeant, doing up his belt. "I must leave Teddy a note. He can't bear it if I go out without a word."

He sat down at the desk and wrote something on a scrap of paper. Then he quietly opened the door to the next room. It was silent and dark in there. Walking on tiptoes, to avoid waking his son, he crept over to the table. But what was this? A note? He looked at the bed in the pale dawn light and saw... Yes! Teddy's bed was empty!

The sergeant threw aside the crumpled quilt. No one there. He swept the whole room with a single glance. Teddy's clothes and shoes were also gone, but right by the window, clearly thrown there in haste, lay his grey socks. The sergeant brought the note over to the light and read:

DEAR DAD, I HEREBY REPORT THAT OPERATION 'CLEMENTINE' HAS BEGUN. I AM GOING WITH PICKLES HE HAS A NOSE LIKE AT SKOTLANDYARD. IN CASE OF NOTHING, SEND CANINE REINFORCEMENTS. BYE, TEDDY.

"What the devil!" An oath completely unsuitable for a police sergeant escaped from Beeper's lips. "I'll show him Scotland Yard! I'll give him an 'operation'! So that's why he was so keen to watch that TV series! Just wait until he gets home!"

The sergeant screwed up Teddy's brilliant report in a fury. He clenched his fists and ran out of the room.

"What's happened?" asked Podger, shocked by his sergeant's pale face.

"Teddy's lost!"

"What do you mean, lost? Where? In his room?"

"Not in his room!" said the sergeant, losing his temper. "In the forest!"

"I don't understand at all!" The constable shook his head. "He's lost in the forest as well? Along with the little girl?"

"No, not with her, but on his own!" said the sergeant, impatiently stuffing his arm into his grey coat sleeve. "Here! Read this!"

Constable Podger carefully examined the piece of paper.

"Wow..." He whistled through his teeth, but immediately stopped and cast an anxious glance at his boss.

"Well, fancy that! What a smarty-pants! When did he leave? In the night?"

"It must have been right after the phone call. He reads too many of those... crime novels! Then he starts fantasizing about Scotland Yard! Except that he can't even spell it properly. What does 'in case of nothing' mean? I'll show him! Come on, let's go, Podger," panted the sergeant. "Let's go to the Jamesons' and the Walkers'. Then a few more houses along the road."

As he passed Pickles's kennel, the sergeant shook his head sadly. Now he knew where that dog was. What an insufferable child Teddy could be! At least in a few days he'd be back at school.

The dawn was grey. The sky was clear, without a single cloud. The sergeant and the constable walked briskly, hopping over puddles from time to time. Neither of them noticed the freshness of the air or the first tweets of the dawn chorus. They were hurrying towards the shed, which had served as the garage for the police jeep for a very long time now.

"We'll drive as far as the crossroads," said Sergeant

Beeper, sitting down in the passenger seat. "We'll get out of the jeep there..."

"As far as the highway, you mean?"

"That's right."

"But where has Teddy gone? What do you think? That boy knows the forest inside out..."

"He won't get anything done on his own. That's obvious. Unless he does it by accident..."

The engine growled and the jeep drove out of the shed onto the sandy ground. Expertly manoeuvring the steering wheel, the constable reached the road at last.

"Hey, boss," he suddenly said, almost leaping out of his seat, "maybe that crazy fellow will know something?"

"Which crazy fellow?"

"You know, the one who's living in the forester's lodge! The one who paints toadstools!"

"Ah, Twisk, the painter! We'll see!"

"OK, we're here," said the constable, coming to a halt at the crossroads.

"Run over to Jameson's house. Tell him to fetch his sons and inform the others. And go and see Walker too. They're all to show up here in fifteen minutes."

"Yes, sir!" shouted Podger and ran off between the fences.

The sergeant hopped out of the jeep and crossed the highway. He looked around him. Perfect silence reigned over the forest, broken only by the rare chirping of a woodland bird. The thick, green ferns that had been pressed to the ground by the intensity of the downpour were straightening out their ragged leaves. He glanced impatiently at his watch. How late it was! All because of Podger's unfortunate accident.

He heard voices in the distance, so ignoring the mud he went back to the road. Someone flashed a torch.

"Five volunteers reporting for duty," said Podger.

"That's not many," grumbled Sergeant Beeper.

"There are more coming—they're just dawdling at home. No one likes traipsing around at night."

"So who are we looking for?" asked one of the volunteers, wrapping his coat more tightly about him.

"Podger said it was a child... a little girl," replied a second, sleepily.

"Come along now! Off to the forest!" ordered Sergeant Beeper.

FIVE VOLUNTEERS

"Which way should we go?"

"Towards the copse, but search the bushes thoroughly..."

"The rest are on their way," said Jameson, panting. "I'll take them to the left, you others go right, in line formation...."

"OK. We'll meet near the forester's lodge. If you find the child, come back to the village with her, and send someone to let us know," replied Beeper.

"Right-o!" said Jameson. "Good luck!"

"It's so muddy!" sighed Beeper and set off.

"I'm already covered in muck!" said the constable, laughing at the memory of his nocturnal bath in the ditch.

They marched along, looking attentively to either side. The forest grew denser. Here and there they could see damage caused by the storm. Broken branches hung from the trees, and a lightning bolt had split the trunk of a huge oak tree down the middle. Further ahead, on the right, a pine tree lay toppled across the path, displaying its knotted network of ripped-up roots.

"Devil take it!" hissed the constable, tripping over a root. "Hey, what is it?" he asked, stopping moments later and looking anxiously at his boss, who was staring upwards, goggle-eyed.

"Look! Up there. There on the left, on the branch..."

"It's something red! What can it be?"

The sergeant was off at a run, ignoring the boggy ground.

"It's a scarf!" he shouted. "A lady's headscarf!"

"All right," muttered Podger, "but why is it so big?"

"Someone must have found the child," said Beeper, removing the red cloth from the branch with a stick.

"How do you know?" asked Podger.

"How else would this scarf have got up there? Eh? The only possible answer is that someone was giving the child a piggyback!"

"What? I don't understand."

"It's simple. Someone has found or kidnapped the child and went past here carrying her on their shoulders. That's why the girl's head was so high up! The scarf she was wearing on her head got caught up in the branches and... stayed in the tree."

"But look how big it is! It can't be a child's scarf. She'd have to have a head the size of a... a mill wheel!" said the constable, turning the red cloth in his hands.

"Yes. You're right. There's something odd about it..." said the sergeant, carefully examining the grass around the foot of the tree. "Podger, look here!"

"Where, Sergeant?"

"Here! On the ground—do you see?"

"Oh my!" gasped the constable, staring with wide-open eyes at the clay-like, boggy ground. "That's... that's... what is that?"

"Footprints, Podger! Footprints! Very strange footprints!"

"Quite so!" said the constable, kneeling down and bending his head low to the ground. There in the wet earth he could see the deep imprints of some enormous feet.

"Maybe it's a yeti!" said the sergeant, laughing.

"A what?" asked one of the villagers in surprise.

"That abominable snowman the papers are always writing about."

"Hey, you're talking nonsense, sir," said Podger, indignantly. "What a thing to say at a time like this! But seriously, whose footprints are these?"

The sergeant parted the branches and set off, lighting his way with the torch. The constable glided along right behind him. Both of them had their gaze fixed on the imprints, which led straight along the left-hand side of the path, avoiding the undergrowth.

From time to time the tracks disappeared on harder soil, and then reappeared in the muddy earth and flattened grass. Broken branches and crushed bushes accompanied the strange footprints.

"Sergeant," whispered Podger at one point. "There are clearly four feet here!"

"Have you found something?" asked one of the village boys, who had met up with them from the left.

"There's something here. Some sort of footprints. I've never seen anything like it," said Walker, scratching his head. "And that's a fact. It's not a cow, and not a horse..."

"But it's not human either!" said Podger, authoritatively.

Up in a tree, a bird began to warble softly. They all raised their heads.

"We'll keep going then," said Walker, and set off to the right.

"Hey! Hey over there!" came the sound of someone calling from afar. "Hey! Waaait!"

"All right, all right, don't yell like that!" shouted back one of the villagers. "It's the Paulsons' boy."

The boy reached them out of breath, and grabbed the sergeant by the sleeve.

"Well? What's happened?"

"They told me to run here," he said, puffing from the effort. "Mrs Bobbin came rushing over to the police station because she found a child..."

"Where did she find her?" asked the constable joyfully.

"Under the quilt!"

"Don't you start fooling around!" muttered an old villager, shaking his fist.

"But that's what Mrs Bobbin said, and they told me to run to you at the double..."

"All right," said Beeper. "We're going back!"

They reached the highway in silence. Day was breaking. On the horizon the sun was rising with a pink glow. They got into the jeep, taking the boy with them. The constable switched on the engine and skilfully turned around towards the police station. The sergeant unbuttoned his coat. It was getting warm. The first rays of sunlight were causing steam to rise from the damp earth. They reached their destination.

"Mr Beeper, sir! Please wait!"

The sergeant turned around and saw the plump Mrs Bobbin from the cottage at the edge of the village, wobbling comically as she pulled along a little girl in a red dress. It was a very funny sight, because in her haste Mrs Bobbin, whom the holidaymakers called Mrs Clotted Cream, had evidently forgotten to wind her grey hair into a bun, and had two little plaits sticking out on either side of her head, which looked like mouse tails.

"Mr Beeper, I mean... Sergeant..." she panted. "Just look... look what I found at home..."

Mrs Bobbin pointed a chubby hand at the little girl, who was staring at the two uniformed officers of the law with terror in her enormous eyes.

"Where did you find her?!"

"But I told you, in my house. In bed..."

"In bed?" said Podger in surprise. "In your bed?"

The constable was speechless. Well, it's not all that often that you find a strange child in your own bed!

"No! In the room I rent to the holidaymakers! I go in there this morning, because I can hear someone crying... and I can't believe my eyes. There's this little one in Annie's bed, and she's got tears rolling down her face like peas! And as for my kiddies... not a trace! I can't get a word out of her! She just sits and stares with those peepers... I ask: where's Annie, where's Mark and the little one? No reply! She just cries and cries... Poor little thing..." said Mrs Bobbin tenderly, wiping her teary eyes. "She must have lost her way and ended up in my house..."

"But how? How did she get in?" asked the sergeant.

Podger stepped closer and knelt down beside the child, who was gazing at him with eyes as blue as the sky.

"So, my dear, tell us, who are you?"

"A little girl," she whispered and stuck a dirty finger in her mouth.

"But what's your name?"

"Macadamia."

"What a strange name," mused the sergeant. "Maybe this is our missing person! But the little girl who was lost in the forest had a different name! And how could she have ended up in a stranger's house, in bed?"

"I don't understand either," the constable agreed.

"Well, she's not from around here," said Mrs Bobbin, shaking her plaits. "Our lot, the holidaymakers, I know them all. I bring them cream and eggs, so I know who lives where. I know all the nippers. But this girl's not been here before."

"In any case," said the sergeant, "we need to report that we've found a child, regardless of whether it's the right one or a different girl. Come to my place, Constable, and we'll try to call by telephone again. I didn't have a chance to tell you that the wretched phone started ringing again when you were on the road. They may have fixed it by now." Then he turned to Mrs Bobbin and said: "Please take the little girl back home with you for now, feed her, give her a bath... We'll come and fetch her later."

"Right you are," said the woman, laughing. "She's as muddy as a duck pond! But... where are my kids? They've never left the house this early before. They didn't even want to get up early to go mushroom-picking. What am I going to tell their parents?"

"Maybe they're hiding? Maybe it's a silly prank?"

Mrs Bobbin bent down and took the little girl by the hand. Macadamia snuggled up to her and yawned deeply.

"Poor little thing," said the constable. "But she's not called Clementine!"

'RIGHT YOU ARE,' SAID THE WOMAN, LAUGHING

"Indeed. On the phone they said it several times loud and clear: Clementine. But this one has a weird name. Macadamia... What will those parents think of next?!"

* * * *

The telephone was still silent.

"Hell and a false leg!" said the sergeant angrily, because he wanted to inform the main police station as soon as possible. "Let's go. I hope everything will finally become clear when we reach the town."

"Should I call off the search in the forest?"

"Maybe not. What if this isn't the right little girl?"

"We'll see."

The constable sat down behind the wheel of the muddy jeep again.

The sergeant reached into the pocket of his uniform and took out the red scarf they'd found in the forest.

"I wonder if that little girl has anything to do with this."

"Do you think so?" asked Podger, stopping in front of Mrs Bobbin's garden gate.

"It's not impossible. But it could be a false trail."

12.

In which we finally find
Clementine and...

===

MR IGNATIUS PROSSER WAS SITTING BY A ROADSIDE
ditch with his head in his hands, in a gesture of utter
helplessness. The cause of his never-ending worries—his
nightmare of a car—was sitting calmly in the middle
of the road, mud-spattered, motionless, with the odd
bit of red paint glittering through, as if laughing at
its owner's despair. And to cap it all... it wasn't even
sneezing any more!

Finally, it had simply come to a halt, and despite Mr
Prosser's desperate efforts, it wouldn't budge an inch. It
was just as though the car wasn't an inanimate object
that did as it was told, but rather lived a life of its own,
with its own moods and spitefulness.

Because the little red car was spiteful! It had kept going fairly well during the nocturnal storm; it had let him drive out of town without any complaints, and they had been so very close to the haven of Mr Twisk's lodge—when suddenly it had stopped!

Mr Prosser rubbed his bristly chin. The mental image of Twisk tucking into his breakfast was unbearable!

"Drat!" he cried, punching himself hard on the knee. "And double drat! I swear, as soon as I get home, I'm taking this car to the scrapyard!" he hissed, casting a look of loathing at the red bonnet.

He was growing more and more tired of this journey into the unknown. Well, it was hardly surprising! The night, which fortunately was over, had hardly been a pleasant one. And to make it worse, he'd slept through the vital moment—when the police van had left to look for the child. Mr Prosser pulled on his jacket. It was still damp. His open umbrella was also drying out in the first, hesitant rays of the rising sun. The day looked set to be warm and fine. The birds, since being silenced by the storm and the darkness of the night, were just waking up, chirping softly. Drops of water were still dripping one by one from the branches of the old oak and beech trees, twinkling merrily in the sunshine. It would actually be lovely to be here on this quiet, secluded forest track, if it weren't for... well, quite—if it weren't for the car!

"What am I to do?" Mr Prosser asked himself the same question for the hundredth time, a question neither he nor anyone else could answer sensibly. Finally, he stood up from the grass, brushed off his crumpled and still damp trousers, folded the umbrella and slowly approached the little red horror.

"Go on, move!" he implored it, taking his seat behind the steering wheel. "Just drive a little bit further, and then you can stop and never move again!"

Ah, if only Mr Prosser had known what he was letting himself in for, addressing the spiteful vehicle in that tone!

But what was this? Once again, a sort of miracle occurred on the forest road, because the ignition burbled as soon as it was switched on, then growled like a very angry dog, and the car took off so suddenly that Mr Prosser only just managed to swerve sharply to the right, narrowly avoiding the thick trunk of a roadside tree.

"Crazy!" he muttered, adjusting his position. "Completely crazy!"

This rather unkind epithet was, of course, directed at the vehicle, which with its truly unhinged behaviour could push anyone, even a much less nervous owner, to the brink.

The road that Mr Prosser was now driving down was leading him into the heart of the increasingly dense forest. On both sides, little spruce trees were turning green, and drops of dew twinkling on their thick, spiky brushes.

"I think I'm supposed to turn off somewhere around here," thought Mr Prosser, slowing down. The road seemed to widen and the forest gave way, revealing a sparse coppice, which the blossoming heather had turned completely lilac. The sight was so lovely that the reporter very nearly stopped the car to enjoy the beauty of the late-summer colours in silence, but then suddenly remembered the spiteful nature of the car he was driving. "It might never move again!" he thought, and doubled his speed. Once again he was surrounded by forest and trees intertwining their branches above him, blocking out the blue dawn sky. He was driving so fast that he only realized at the very last moment that there was something in this remote patch of forest that was completely incomprehensible and out of place.

Because there on the narrow road, still damp from the night-time rain, stood... an elephant.

That's right, a real live elephant, as big as a barn, with large grey ears that it was flapping rhythmically to and fro, to and fro...

Mr Prosser, who had only just managed to come to a halt right behind its back legs as thick as pillars, stared in amazement at the rolls of dark-grey skin and the tiny tail that the great beast was waving cheerfully. The elephant was standing on the path with its back to Mr Prosser, and clearly had no intention of going any further. It looked as if it had been standing in this strange forest for ages, and as if it found this a particularly enjoyable thing to do.

Mr Prosser completely lost his head. What was an elephant doing in the forest? He was after all a conscious human being, and what he was seeing before him was not a bizarre dream! Mr Prosser did occasionally have strange and terrible dreams, mostly involving flocks of white sheep, but an elephant? No, never an elephant! In any case, this animal was actually real. It was moving its ears and tail, and now it was even… raising its trunk and snapping off a twig from an acacia tree.

"I'll have to scare it away somehow, to drive it off this narrow road, or I'll be stuck here for as long as it pleases to stay!"

Without thinking too hard about it, Mr Prosser honked his horn and its harsh, blaring noise suddenly pierced the entire forest. The elephant twitched, waved its ears anxiously, then turned its head to look behind it, closed its little eyes, which were buried in thick folds of skin, took a step backwards and suddenly, quite unexpectedly… sat down with the whole weight of its elephantine body on the bonnet of the little red car!

That was just too much for Mr Prosser's feeble nerves! Hearing the scrunch of the bonnet as it was crushed flat, first he closed his eyes tight shut, then opened them wide, but the sight of the elephant sitting comfortably on his bonnet had not disappeared. Just the opposite! Quite unharmed by the squashed metal, the elephant had turned its head to look at him, as though expecting something!

The look in its tiny eyes was somewhere between surprise and enquiry...

Mr Prosser clutched at his temples and gave a loud groan. Well, the sight was truly bizarre: the little red car, or rather what was left of it, and the great, magnificent grey elephant waving its ears in a friendly way...

At that moment a police jeep appeared on the forest road, screeching to a halt right behind the red-and-grey obstacle.

"Clementine!" squealed Macadamia, leaping out of the car and racing towards the elephant.

"Careful!" cried Constable Podger, struggling to extract his long legs from the jeep.

"So that's the mysterious Clementine!" exclaimed Sergeant Beeper, laughing hard enough to bring tears to his eyes.

Meanwhile Macadamia had pressed herself against the elephant, and, stretching up on tiptoes, was kissing it, joyfully whispering, "Clementine! My lovely Clementine!"

AS THOUGH
EXPECTING SOMETHING!

The elephant cautiously stood up, raised its head and trumpeted joyfully, sending an echo right round the forest. Then it bent down, wrapped its trunk around the little girl, and with a precision worthy of the most fabulous circus performance, placed her on its back.

Constable Podger was standing next to the car, gazing in astonishment at the crumpled bonnet.

"Excuse me, sir..." whispered Mr Prosser, tugging at the constable's sleeve. "What exactly is going on here? My car..."

And indeed, Mr Prosser's car presented what is commonly called the picture of misery and despair. In fact, it didn't really exist any more, or rather its front end didn't exist. Sergeant Beeper had finally stepped out of the police jeep and was carefully examining the red wreckage.

"Well, I'm blowed..." he whispered, walking around the car accompanied by the completely flabbergasted journalist. "I can't think why it did that."

Mr Prosser seemed to be regaining his composure. After the initial shock came the appropriate reaction, and suddenly, to the surprise of all those present, Mr Prosser sat down on his heels and roared with wonderful, healthy laughter!

"Oh, she was an old banger!" he cackled. "I told her earlier that if she went just a little bit further, she could stop and never move again!"

"Who did you tell, sir?" asked Constable Podger, uncertainly.

"You know... the car..." Mr Prosser was chuckling so much that his cheeks were quivering with laughter.

"Just look at that! Oh my! What on earth is going on?" they suddenly heard someone exclaim, and all turned around in unison.

Teddy and Annie stepped out from between the trees and onto the road. Then Pickles leapt out behind them, panting, and stopping short at the sight of the elephant he dug his four paws into the ground.

"Teddy! What are you doing here? I've been terribly worried about you!" cried the sergeant, stroking his son's tousled hair.

"Dad, this is Annie, I found her in the forest and I thought she was Clementine... you know, the girl you were meant to be looking for..." explained the boy.

"That's Clementine!" said the sergeant, pointing at the elephant.

"That's meant to be Clementine?!" cried Teddy and Annie simultaneously, looking at each other in surprise. "But it was a child that went missing, a little girl..."

"There's been an awful kerfuffle," muttered the sergeant. "But it's all ended well. Our missing child is currently sitting on Clementine's back!"

"But that's Macadamia," said Annie, waving her hands, "the little girl we found yesterday! She said she had lost Clementine in the forest, so we—"

"So you thought Clementine was another little girl, right?"

"That's right," whispered Annie, rubbing the tip of her dirty nose.

"And you went into the forest at night to look for her," said Constable Podger.

"Yes. With Mark and Pudding."

"And where are they now?" asked the sergeant, uneasily.

"They went missing during the storm," said Teddy.

"Maybe they went to the forester's lodge?" piped up Mr Prosser. "I was just on my way there, when—"

"Now that's a thought!" cried the constable. "I'll drive over there, and on the way I'll call off the search..."

"Yes. Everyone can go back to the village. They got up at the crack of dawn, after all..."

"Please tell Mr Twisk that I can't get there, because—"

"Because an elephant sat on your car!" said Sergeant Beeper, laughing loudly.

"Yes, and a good thing too—the car was already on its last legs!" cackled Mr Prosser, waving his arms about like a windmill.

"But why? Why did it sit down?" asked Annie and Teddy in chorus, staring in dumbstruck surprise at the great big elephant, which had carefully removed Macadamia from its back and gently set her down.

"That we don't know," replied the sergeant.

"Do you know who she is, sir?" asked Annie, pointing to Macadamia.

"She's the circus director's daughter..."

"The circus?" said Teddy in amazement.

"What circus?" asked Annie.

"A circus has come to town on tour. Macadamia will be performing with her partner... Clementine."

"Oh, if only I hadn't driven to town!" sighed Mr Prosser. "Perhaps I'd have found this elephant sooner and nobody would have had to spend the night rummaging about in the forest... All I can do now is to write an article about it!"

"And yesterday evening," continued the sergeant, "at one of their stopovers not far from St Jude's, Clementine walked off unnoticed into the forest. Macadamia ran after her, and then they both went missing. The circus company aren't familiar with these parts, so they called the police. But they didn't know that it was closer to the police station in St Jude's than the one in town!"

"And we thought there were two little girls!" said Annie laughing, her white teeth twinkling in her terribly grimy face.

"I didn't really know who I was looking for either," admitted the sergeant, sitting down on a tree stump. "It was only when Mrs Bobbin brought us that little girl, saying she had found her in her house instead of the children she was supposed to be looking after—"

"Mrs Bobbin?" said Annie, laughing. "We call her Mrs Clotted Cream! She must have had a fine look on her face, I bet!"

"She did indeed!" The sergeant tried to give her a stern look, but burst out laughing instead.

Annie was so grimy and dirty from hiding in the hollow and sleeping in the hut that the sight of her was bound to make anyone laugh.

"She did indeed," repeated the sergeant. "But did it even occur to you how very worried everyone would be?"

"That's why we left Freddie and Eddie on guard!" mumbled Annie, realizing that perhaps it hadn't been such a reasonable solution after all. "They were supposed to look after Macadamia..."

"But they went off too and left me on my own!" squealed Macadamia, cuddling up to a thick elephant leg.

"Where did they go?" cried Annie and the sergeant in chorus.

"To the forest... to look for her..." said the child, pointing at the elephant.

"This is just too much!" said the sergeant, clutching his brow. "Instead of looking for one child, now I have to find four!"

"Then I'll go!" said Teddy, leaping to his feet. Hearing his cry, Pickles, lying low until now, pricked up his ears.

"You're not going anywhere!" yelled the sergeant. "You've caused me more than enough worry already!"

"But I left you a report—" said Teddy, indignantly.

"You call that a report?" said the sergeant with a frown. "You even misspelt 'Scotland Yard'! And what was 'in case of nothing, send canine reinforcements' supposed to mean?" the sergeant mocked him mercilessly.

Teddy hung his head. He was highly ashamed of those mistakes, which he had absolutely no recollection of making. But he was even more ashamed that Dad had said it in front of Annie...

"All right, that's enough," said the sergeant, glancing at Teddy's drooping head. "I'm sure you'll grow up to be a brilliant detective!"

"But I did find her!" said Teddy, pointing at Annie.

"What will happen to Mark and Pudding?" said Annie.

"We'll find them all," promised the sergeant, standing up from the tree stump.

They heard the rumble of an approaching car in the distance.

"That must be the constable on his way back," said Mr Prosser, rousing himself and quickly getting up.

The rumble of the engine was ever closer and louder. Finally, the jeep came around the corner and in it they saw... Mr Twisk, Mark, Freddie, Eddie and little Pudding, who was already shrieking at the sight of the elephant.

"Wow! It's Babar the Elephant!"

The jeep stopped at the roadside and all the children spilt out of it like pears from a basket.

"Annie! I thought you were lost!"

"Pudding, you poor little thing, were you very afraid?"

"It was gggreat," babbled Pudding, cautiously approaching the elephant. "I kept having to rescue Mark, and we were very nearly eaten by a wolf!"

"A wolf? What wolf?" asked Teddy. "There aren't any wolves around here!"

"There weren't any elephants either, but there's one here now," protested Pudding, staring goggle-eyed at the elephant's huge ears.

"The constable told us who Clementine is," said Mark. "What a lark!"

"And I'm telling you, there are no wolves here," insisted Teddy, scratching good old Pickles behind the ear. The dog was quietly growling at the elephant, but keeping his distance just to be on the safe side.

"If there aren't any wolves, whose eyes did we see shining in the dark?"

"Where?" asked Teddy.

"There, above our pit, the one we fell into!"

"Now I know," said Teddy, nodding. "That was... Pickles!"

"Pickles? Pickles with what?" said Mark in surprise.

"My dog," said Teddy, laughing. "He ran away in the forest, and that must have been when he found your pit! We were there later on, but there was nobody in it any more. Annie thought it must be a bear's den!"

"Annie, why are you so dirty?"

"Because she was sitting in a hollow and there were loads of woodchips, and when I saw her, she was glowing all over," explained Teddy.

"Glowing?" asked Freddie, confused.

"Yes, because rotting woodchips glow in the dark. Didn't you know that?" said Eddie, shrugging, and walked over to Mr Twisk, who was having a lively conversation with Mr Prosser by the remains of the car.

"I just don't understand," Mr Twisk was saying. "She's completely destroyed your car!"

"It's no great loss," replied Mr Prosser. "What's more, I'll be able to write a brilliant article!"

"Will you write about us too, sir?" asked Freddie. He knew by now that the longed-for medal was a lost cause, but if his surname appeared in the newspapers, then he'd still be a hero! At least for his friends at school!

"I'll write about you, and it," said Mr Prosser, pointing at the elephant, who was calmly munching on acacia leaves.

"About her, I think you mean—about Clementine," Annie corrected him.

"That's a lady elephant," said Mark solemnly.

"Of course, it was 'Operation Clementine', after all!"

"The operation is over," said the sergeant. "Are any children still missing?"

"No!" they shouted in chorus.

"Just as well," muttered Mr Twisk under his breath. He was really starting to feel the effects of the disturbed night.

In the distance they heard the rumble of another car. This time it was coming from the opposite direction. Everyone jumped to their feet, curious to see who was approaching.

"I hope it's the lads," muttered the sergeant to Constable Podger. "From the police station!"

A small green car appeared from between the trees.

A stout man in a stripy vest leapt out of it. Behind him came Sergeant Whiskers and Constable Muggins.

"Daddy!" squealed Macadamia and raced towards the car.

"My daughter! She's been found!" cried the newcomer, sweeping the little girl into his arms.

The four police officers exchanged glances and sighed with relief.

"Call off the search," said Sergeant Whiskers to Constable Muggins, wiping the sweat from his brow. "It's been going on all night..."

"We were combing the forest too, but the children must have been at the forester's lodge by then—"

"And we were in the hut!" interrupted Teddy.

Now everybody went over to the car. Clementine clearly recognized her master's voice, because she suddenly trumpeted so loudly that the forest birds fell silent.

"I am Henry MacAdam, circus director," said the fat man, holding out a hand the size of a loaf of bread to

A HAND THE SIZE OF A LOAF OF BREAD

Sergeant Beeper. "From the bottom of my heart, thank you for helping to find my little girl."

"We weren't able to do much," explained Sergeant Whiskers. "The storm prevented us. I don't even know," he said, turning to his colleagues from St Jude's, "if you understood anything from our phone conversation. They're only fixing the line now."

"That wretched storm!" snarled Constable Podger. "We couldn't hear a thing. Just the name, Clementine..."

"Hey," whispered Eddie to Freddie. "Now I understand what the prehistoric animal was that I saw flashing by in the forest! What a lark!"

"Was it the elephant?" asked Mr Prosser with a smile, carefully making notes.

"In the forest," said Sergeant Beeper, "we found a red headscarf high up in a tree, and footprints... very strange, enormous footprints..."

"We thought it was a yeti!" said the constable, laughing.

"Of course, it was Clementine who lost the head-scarf," explained Mr MacAdam. "She wears it during performances and rehearsals. It must have got caught on a branch."

"And she really does have a head the size of a mill wheel!" said Constable Podger, examining the elephant.

"The most important thing is that we've found Molly," said the director, happily.

"Who's Molly?" asked the children in chorus. "She said her name was Macadamia!"

"That's what the circus folk call her!" said the director, laughing. "It comes from my surname, MacAdam... But hang on, what's this?" he cried, noticing the crumpled car. "This must be Clementine's doing!"

"But why? Perhaps you can explain why she did that?" asked Mr Prosser.

"I know why," he said. "It's quite simple. In our circus show, Clementine has her own special number..."

"Special number?" asked Pudding.

"That's what it's called," explained the director. "It's one of the circus acts. At the end of it, when Clementine puts Molly back on the ground, a specially constructed red car comes on stage..."

"I see," whispered Mr Prosser, noting something down.

"And at the sound of the horn, the elephant sits on the car and drives off into the wings."

"And I honked the horn to chase her out of the way!" said Mr Prosser.

"So the elephant saw the red car..." cackled the constable, slapping his knee.

"And sat down!" cried the children, bursting into laughter.

"What a lark!" said Freddie, stamping his feet with delight.

"I would be most willing to cover the costs of repairing your car, sir," said Mr MacAdam graciously.

"Not in a million years!" cried Mr Prosser, waving his umbrella about. "This car has ruined my health and my nerves!"

"In which case I would like to invite all those present to a performance at the circus this evening!"

"Brilliant! Hooray! Fantastic!" cried the children.

"We'll give you a lift into town," said Sergeant Beeper, patting Pudding on the head.

"What a shame the holidays are nearly over," sighed Eddie.

"And the school term is starting soon," moaned Freddie.

"But you've had your great big adventure," replied

Phosphorus Twisk, sucking on his pipe although it had gone out.

"And your major operation," added Sergeant Beeper, smiling knowingly at Teddy.

"And now you're all invited to my house for fried wild mushrooms," said Mr Twisk, taking the journalist by the arm. "We can have a nice stroll through the forest."

"And you can make some delicious scrambled eggs," said Mr Prosser dreamily, feeling his stomach rumbling.

...SUCKING ON HIS PIPE ALTHOUGH IT HAD GONE OUT...

The children set off eagerly down the path. The adults walked behind them, and at the rear came Clementine with the blissful Molly—Macadamia on her back. Both cars were left on the road, so that after breakfast they could tow the pitiful remains of the third one back to town.

"Annie," said Pudding, looking back at the elephant, "would you... would you want to have huuuuge ears like Clementine's?"

"Yes, I would," said the little girl, "because then I'd be able to hear everything perfectly..."

"Well, I wouldn't," said Pudding solemnly, "because it'd take me forever to wash them!"

THE END